Cadillac
Cathedral

OTHER BOOKS BY
JACK HODGINS

Spit Delaney's Island (1976)

The Invention of the World (1977)

The Resurrection of Joseph Bourne (1979)

The Barclay Family Theatre (1981)

The Honorary Patron (1987)

Left Behind in Squabble Bay (1988)

Innocent Cities (1990)

Over Forty in Broken Hill (1992)

A Passion for Narrative: A Guide to Writing Fiction
(1993, expanded 2001)

The Macken Charm (1995)

Broken Ground (1998)

Distance (2003)

Damage Done by the Storm (2004)

The Master of Happy Endings (2010)

Cadillac
Cathedral

❧

A TALE

Jack Hodgins

RONSDALE PRESS

CADILLAC CATHEDRAL
Copyright © 2014 Jack Hodgins

RONSDALE PRESS
3350 West 21st Avenue
Vancouver, B.C. Canada V6S 1G7
www.ronsdalepress.com

Typesetting: Julie Cochrane, in Granjon 11.5 pt on 17
Cover Design: David Drummond
Paper: Ancient Forest Friendly Silva, FSC Recycled, 100% post-consumer waste, totally chlorine-free and acid-free.

Ronsdale Press wishes to thank the following for their support of its publishing program: the Canada Council for the Arts, the Government of Canada through the Canada Book Fund, the British Columbia Arts Council, and the Province of British Columbia through the British Columbia Book Publishing Tax Credit program.

Library and Archives Canada Cataloguing in Publication

Hodgins, Jack, 1938–, author
  Cadillac cathedral / Jack Hodgins.

Issued in print and electronic formats.
ISBN 978-1-55380-298-3 (print)
ISBN 978-1-55380-300-3 (ebook) / ISBN 978-1-55380-299-0 (pdf)

  I. Title.

PS8565.O3C33 2014   C813'.54   C2013-906857-0   C2013-906858-9

At Ronsdale Press we are committed to protecting the environment. To this end we are working with Canopy (formerly Markets Initiative) and printers to phase out our use of paper produced from ancient forests. This book is one step towards that goal.

Printed in Canada by Marquis Book Printing, Quebec

for
Lauren, Dexter, Emmett

ACKNOWLEDGEMENTS

The author is grateful to the *Chor Leoni* Men's Choir, Erick Lichte, and the late Diane Loomer for encouraging and producing a collaborative song-and-narrative performance based on an early version of this story.

The people, events, and places in this story are fictional. The community of Portuguese Creek is not to be confused with a real Vancouver Island community visited by a creek of that name.

Cadillac
Cathedral

CHAPTER 1

⌘

HE WAS A MAN in his seventies whose retirement years were filled with the pleasure of restoring cars and trucks that had been wrecked and then abandoned by those who could afford to replace them. From mountain roads and vacant lots he towed them home and got them running again for those who could not afford something off a used-car dealer's yard. Having felt the frosty breath of old age on the back of his neck now and then, Arvo Saarikoski found pleasure in rebuilding old cars to something like their former selves — a miracle he could hardly manage for himself.

When friends suggested he take the opportunity to travel before he got too old, he waved the notion aside. He'd travelled *already* —

New Orleans, San Francisco, twice to the Baltic countries. Travel was exhausting, crowds were confusing, foreign countries were determined to empty your bank account. Worse, being carted around from place to place made him feel useless. He hadn't been allowed to give the Norwegian tour bus a badly needed tune-up. He'd been prevented from examining the engine of the Louisiana paddle-wheeler, though he could tell it was in serious trouble while they laboured up a steamy canal.

Since he was determined not to travel any more, neighbours recommended a night-school class for seniors. It was never too late to learn something new. Bee-keeping. Photography. The history of labour unions. But he didn't *need* a night-school class! Arvo was satisfied with what he was doing — what he'd been doing for years. You could see the results out there on the roads. A handsome '38 Ford V8 he'd rebuilt for the elderly Gordon twins was still being driven in vintage car parades by the one surviving sister. A '93 Saturn, once inhabited by a family of raccoons in a derelict barn, now carried Colin Hardy and his classmates to and from the college south of town. Arvo had worked for a month and a half on the 1982 Camaro he'd found overturned in a gravel pit behind Connor Lake, determined to get it ready for Tom Grove's high school graduation. He'd been rewarded with a kiss from the girlfriend and an invitation to attend the ceremony — though once he'd dressed in his suit and tie he'd decided the invitation had been only a courtesy, not meant to be taken seriously.

From wrecks that defied his efforts to revive them, he salvaged the reusable parts and hauled the carcasses onto the field behind his house. Since Portuguese Creek was eleven kilometres north of town, there were no officials to object to his sprawling graveyard of auto parts.

Nor was there a wife to object to this view from the kitchen window. He had survived a few close-calls that might have surprised his friends if they'd known. It had been mostly married women who'd found this loose-limbed lanky bachelor intriguing. But he'd seen how these women frowned at the crescents of grease beneath his fingernails and knew they were plotting to clean him up and suggest a different sort of activity to fill his days. When he'd dropped hints of a broken heart that had never completely mended, they'd decided not to waste their time on a man who would rather restore life to old cars than reawaken passion in an ageing woman's heart.

At any rate, he suspected that any woman who saw the inside of his house would be alarmed to see how perfect he'd been keeping it. He might labour with engines and oily car parts in his workshop but he never failed to scrub down in his backyard sauna before returning to the house he kept as spotless as his mother had kept it before him. You could see yourself reflected in her linoleum floors; you saw no unwashed dishes in her kitchen sink nor wrinkle in the satin cover on his bed. Her crocheted doilies remained stiff with starch and perfectly white beneath the family photos on her polished tables. A day in the grease pit did not prevent him from keeping the place just as Silvi Saarikoski had famously kept it before him.

Few had forgotten the heavy middle-aged woman from Thunder Bay who had stepped down off a bus claiming in the Store to be his "intended." This was almost twenty years ago. No one but Arvo had known she'd arrived as the result of a letter he'd written — unwisely, it turned out. She had not been intimidated by his meticulous housekeeping, nor was she bothered by his love affair with old cars, but within the month he'd found good reason to put both her and her teenaged son onto another bus.

Of course the next time Arvo put foot inside the Store, Matt

Foreman suggested that Thunder Bay was a long way to come for such a short visit.

"I would've liked it even shorter," Arvo said. "Turned out she was mostly looking for someone to bail her light-fingered son out of jail every weekend."

Foreman removed a few outdated notices from the cork-board above the coffee maker. "I thought I heard her yelling Finnish at you once."

Arvo laughed. "Her *suomeski* wasn't much better than mine but she knew more swear words than my Uncle Ahti. I heard just about every one of them while I was pushing her onto the bus. She cursed me even while I was paying for their tickets! Turned out the whole business cost me more than I knew — as I found out next time I went to my underwear drawer for some cash."

"She robbed you?"

"You could say she taught me a lesson."

"Not to give up on women altogether?"

"To give up on any woman I met since I was twenty or thirty years old."

He knew that so far as the local wives and widows were concerned, his unhappy experience with the woman from Thunder Bay had served him right. A long-armed, long-legged, long-backed scrawny man who preferred the company of four-wheeled wrecks to the companionship of an affectionate female had no business expecting anything from life but loneliness. If he was worth keeping an eye on at all, it was only because there was a slim possibility they might witness a reunion with his first and only sweetheart, the rumoured mystery girl whose name had not been spoken here but whose existence was never in doubt.

He knew most of what was said about him. Portuguese Creek was a rural community where the people who talked about you behind your back were usually happy to say the same things to your face. He would laugh and brush away their words without a comment, anxious to get back to doing something important, like replacing the brake drum on the Chev pickup he'd found abandoned in Hagan Creek, the spring runoff having risen as high as the shattered windshield.

Most of Arvo's entertaining took place in his workshop on afternoons when friends came down to collect their mail at the Store and crossed the road to his shed of rough planks and corrugated-iron, where the double doors were usually open while he worked. They sat on the stacks of old tires or overturned boxes to complain about the unreliable weather and the traitorous whims of their own untrustworthy bodies. They spoke of fly-wheels and shock absorbers and the gutlessness of certain makes of car, and swore the pot hole in the road past Baileys' gate had got so deep and wide it should be reclassified as a lake and given a name. There were few weeks in a year it wasn't filled with muddy water. Herbie Brewer predicted it would soon be coming through the floorboards and drowning his socks.

Herbie Brewer leaned against a post where he could rub his back on a convenient knot, but Peterson always sat with knees wide apart on an empty mortise-cornered wooden box stamped with faded letters: *CIL Explosives*. Because Arvo would not allow smoking in his workshop, Bert Peterson chewed fiercely at a stick of gum until it lost its flavour, then disposed of the exhausted wad against a side of the box beneath him and fished another stick from the pocket of his long-sleeved faded cotton shirt.

Cynthia O'Brien liked to sit near the open doorway where she could take part in the conversation while breathing air untainted by motor oil and watching the traffic go by. She may have taught mathematics to some of those drivers — every bit as restless then as they appeared to be now. The doorway to Arvo's workshop was a chance for her to observe the world while participating in the sort of conversations she used to hear about from her late husband. Once you've walked up to the Store to get your mail, she'd told Arvo, walking home could be depressing for someone who'd once participated in staff meetings and classroom debates. Women friends tended to feel they had to interrupt what they were doing and make her a cup of tea, but she could count on Arvo to go right on with his work.

For Arvo, whether there were visitors or not, there was always a radiator in need of a flush-out or a tire to replace on a rescued truck. Today they'd arrived when his head was beneath the hood of an early-model Mazda whose engine he'd only begun to take apart. He'd rather chat with friends while working than invite them into the house where he would have to ask them to take off their shoes and be careful where they sat. Inside his house they would expect him to bring out a cake or a cookie jar, and would then drop crumbs on the floor. For this reason he kept a coffee urn at one end of the workbench, beside his stack of crime paperbacks. Visitors could help themselves to a mug of coffee and a cinnamon roll he'd made from his mother's *korvapuustit* recipe and not interrupt his work. A decent mechanic who took his work seriously could keep most vehicles running indefinitely. "Of course, the auto makers would arrange to have you killed if they heard you'd figured out how."

But it was not the auto makers who were on everyone's mind this afternoon, it was Martin Glass. "Too bad the doctors aren't as smart as Arvo," Peterson said. "They might've kept Martin's insides humming a little longer."

But people, unlike automobiles, could not always be reborn with another's rescued parts — not once they'd stopped breathing at least.

Until recently, Martin Glass had been one of the regulars in Arvo's machine shop, a one-term, long-ago Member of Parliament, who'd spoken only two or three times in the House and yet had quietly managed to secure the creation of a national wildlife park here in the valley, tripling the number of visitors to the area every summer and bringing new life to several businesses in town. Of course the town council took most of the credit for this boost to the local economy.

Martin had been an expert on local history he'd learned from his grandfather, one of the veterans who'd settled here after the First World War. He'd known who'd originally cleared each plot of land, could tell which family had built the still-standing houses, and had stories to tell about the fire that came down out of the mountains to wipe out many of their newly completed homes. He remembered when the tiny Anglican Church — stolen from the neighbouring community and dragged up the road behind a tractor — was still being used one Sunday of every month. Martin had even attended a service now and then.

But down in his waterfront home at the foot of Stevenson Road he had been hit quite suddenly with a mysterious ailment that stymied the local doctors, who'd passed him on to a city specialist with a reputation as a miracle-worker. After only three days in the miracle-worker's care, Martin Glass had died.

Now his body waited for someone to make a decision. His friends were aware that there was no one but them to make it — no family except for a son who'd gone off to live in Saskatchewan and not returned, no political colleagues still alive in this part of the world, no close friends but themselves.

"He wouldn't want to be buried down there in the city," Cynthia said. "I can see him kicking up a fuss if they tried."

Bert Peterson agreed. "I can't help but think it'll take a lot more than just being dead to keep Martin from letting you know what he thought."

"Well, *we* know what he thought," Arvo said, coming out from under the Mazda's hood with the fuel pump in his hand. In this summer afternoon warmth he kept his dark blue coveralls unzipped to the waist. Today there were finger smears of grease on the visible ribs of his narrow chest. "We've got to go down and bring the poor man home."

Cynthia's tone was doubtful. "You think doctors'll hand him over just because we say *Please*?"

"I have the paperwork somewhere," Arvo said. He narrowed his eyes and thought hard, looking up at the floating flecks of dust in the light from the high windows. "He got me to sign something years ago. Made me his executor or whatever the hell it's called. That'll be why I was the one they phoned."

"Bless his heart," Cynthia sighed. "He was always thoughtful of others."

"He taught me to swim," Herbie said. Of course they all knew this. When Herbie had arrived to live with Peterson — some sort of distant cousin — Martin had refused to take him out in his little boat until he'd been subjected to a few lessons.

"Those papers say anything about how we're supposed to pick him up?" Peterson asked. "We can't just throw him in the trunk and drive off."

"I'll have to call on what's-his-name in town," Arvo said. "Henderson's funeral outfit." Before placing the Mazda's fuel pump on his workbench he brushed a pair of dead spark plugs into the battered garbage can. "To send them down a hearse."

"There goes Harry Hickson, heading north!" Cynthia announced. "I wonder who he knows in *that* direction. Didn't he take a stab at running against our Martin?"

"Too bad Arvo never built himself a hearse out of all his salvaged parts," Peterson said. "We could've taken care of Martin ourselves."

Arvo dipped both hands in his pan of gasoline and dried them on a discarded pyjama leg. "You think I never rebuilt a hearse?" He lifted his striped engineer cap and relocated it farther back on his thinning hair, then leaned against his workbench and folded his arms. He reminded them of the time the police hired him to haul a rolled-over hearse to the junkyard and he'd brought it here instead. "Fixed it up and sold it to some hippies — back when there were genuine hippies still around."

Well, he knew that a few of them were still around even now, though they couldn't really be called hippies since they'd started working in the construction industry, or managing one of the forest-farms where they do what they like to call "harvesting" trees. The particular group of ex-hippies that had bought the reconditioned hearse had crammed half their tribe inside and driven off to disappear somewhere east — probably in the Rockies.

"The problem is, you don't find many decent wrecks any more," Arvo was sad to report. "Before you can get at them they've been mashed down to the size of a suitcase and sent away for recycling."

"I seen a hearse when I was out grouse-hunting once," Peterson said. "Back in the mountains, up behind McConnell Lake. Looked about as old as the hills behind it."

"You're sure it was a hearse?" Arvo said. He winked at Herbie. "Was it black?"

"Everything on *wheels* was black in those days," Cynthia said. Though she kept her eye on the outside world, she missed nothing that was being said. "I remember seeing my very first coloured car when I was a girl — green! I thought it was some kind of joke."

"Well," Peterson said, "what I seen looked like one of them old-time glass-walled horse-drawn hearses, but with an open-air driver's cab and a long engine hood out front. Running board with spare tire mounted on it."

Silence followed this.

"Isabel Macken's going into the Store," Cynthia reported. "Back from riding horses up the Fraser Canyon. She hasn't broken any limbs that I can see."

"I just might know that hearse you're talking about," Arvo said, aware of an increase in his heart rate but frowning fiercely at his own long hands. "When an undertaker named Birdsong bought himself a modern hearse — this was down in the city, long ago now — I remember he lent the old one to a cousin who'd fallen on hard times. Old Joe Hudson was a butcher who used to deliver his roasts and steaks up and down the highway around here. After he died, nobody knew where it went. He started pacing the length of the workbench, his long narrow face flushed-up. "That hearse you seen is a Cadillac — I'm sure of it. Manufactured by a fellow named Cunningham back in the thirties. I had my hands inside her engine once when Hudson owned her. Where'd you say you saw it?"

"This one don't need much fixing," Peterson said. "Second time I seen it, a family running one of them so-called tree farm outfits was using it."

"Using it for what?" Arvo said, ready to be indignant.

"You sure you want to know?" Peterson said. "It was parked beside a pile of fresh-cut pole-size Douglas fir — a cable shackled to the rear axle."

Though not usually given to sudden outbursts, Arvo slammed his open hand against the nearest post, rattling the iron roof and dislodging dust from the rafters. "What sort of idiot would use a hearse to haul logs?"

No one had an answer to this, though they seemed to be giving it thought.

"Someone needs to rescue that poor thing," Cynthia eventually said — sang it rather, as she tended to do with anything that might sound like advice. She placed her wide-brimmed hat on her head and slapped a hand on the top to nail it in place.

The others waited for more.

"Well?" She huffed up, an impatient classroom teacher again, and shifted to face the men. "What were we just saying? If we got our hands on that hearse we could use her to haul poor Martin to the graveyard! Could we not?"

"We could not," Bert Peterson said. "Why would a hospital turn one of their bodies over to us?"

"Why wouldn't they?" Cynthia snapped back. "Arvo has only to find the paper that says we can. They'll be glad to have someone take Martin off their hands. There's no one else to do it."

This was Cynthia's no-nonsense approach to things — the teacher who'd retired early to run the concession-stand at her husband's drive-in movie theatre long after drive-in movies had gone out of fashion. Anyone who objected to the price of drinks received a lesson in economics. After Henry's death she'd closed the business and let the property go back to its native bush. There were other things for a person to do in life.

She reminded the men that Martin had had no real friends but themselves, at least in the past few years. Even the party officials who'd worked for Martin's election had stopped inviting him to their events, and his name had not appeared in the local paper for years. He'd claimed that this was fine with him — exactly what he preferred.

Arvo remembered Martin saying, "I've had my moment in the sun. Nobody listened to me in Ottawa, so why should anyone listen here?" Rather than shop in town he'd ordered his groceries delivered to his little sea-side place at the end of Cynthia's road. It seemed that most of his recent social life had taken place right here in Arvo's shed.

"Martin would be pleased," Arvo said. "Stealing the hearse, I mean. Instead of just asking Henderson Funerals to go down and pick him up. But he'll be pissed he couldn't be in on it himself."

"Well, he *will* be in on it," Cynthia said. "In a manner of speaking."

Arvo used the pyjama leg to erase his fingerprints from the Mazda's hood. "Let's not get ahead of ourselves," he said. "First we have to find that hearse. Then, if we're going to rescue poor old Martin from that hospital morgue, I'll have to get her into good-enough shape for the trip."

CHAPTER 2

❧

PORTUGUESE CREEK IS A quiet country place of woods and fields spread out along the Old Highway — houses flanked by trees at the head of long driveways, cows grazing in orchards, sleek horses looking over fences at the passing traffic. There is no sign saying "Welcome to Portuguese Creek" or "Thank you for Visiting." Most drivers need neither the welcome nor the gratitude, since the Store is where most of them still have to go for their mail.

The Creek itself begins as a surface leakage from an underground stream and wanders over the district as if it has lost its way or decided to pay a brief visit to every small farm and house-lot before turning west to abandon itself to an inland river. In some places it is not much more than a ditch, choked with weeds and brush; in other spots it is wide and shallow above a sparkling gravel bed, or filthy with the mud stirred up by cattle crossing.

The road past Arvo's house and workshop had originally been a logging railway line, starting down near the beach and working its careful way inland to cross what would later be the highway — now known as the Old Highway — and then to pass between the Store and Arvo's house and several small family farms towards the now-dismantled Company town where Arvo worked for thirty-five years in the machine shop. The railway tracks had been torn up long ago and the roadbed paved over with an inferior sort of asphalt, now crumbling away at the edges.

If they hoped to bring Martin home in that hearse, it was important to hurry up and do this before the hospital authorities decided on some other form of action. An arrangement made over the phone by an unseen executor and "closest friend" may seem less and less official as time went by, and Arvo did not want to drive all the way down to the city only to find that Martin had been released to some local funeral parlour where a stranger would be messing with Martin's future.

Fortunately, they would not have to travel great distances to find what they were after. Bert Peterson remembered that he'd spotted the old hearse up an abandoned logging road behind Sentinel Hill and onto a lower slope of Douglas Mountain. "Well below the snow-line. Probably no more than thirty k from here."

Herbie Brewer muttered "*Miles*." He had been raised in California and believed that mileage was the only legitimate form of measurement on this continent, proclaimed by God Himself while he handed out copies of the US Constitution shortly after the first mountain had risen from the sea.

Peterson ignored Herbie's opinion just as he ignored everything else he considered irrelevant. He was Herbie's only living relative and had inherited his distant cousin after the aunt he'd lived with into his fifties had died and left him alone in a twelve-foot Arizona trailer.

Cynthia would not accompany them into the mountains. A niece had promised to stop in for a visit and she had yet to bake something to serve with tea. She promised, however, that once the men had rescued the hearse and got it ready for travel, she'd have baked a banana loaf for their trip to rescue Martin. "Martin loved my banana loaf."

Arvo suggested her loaf would be wasted on Martin now. "If he's aware of anything at all he'll be busy checking out his new location."

"Still," Cynthia began, but apparently decided against explaining herself. Maybe she thought she'd made a joke and didn't know what to do with his response.

He should not be making light of the matter — referring to Martin's "new location." The fact was, he didn't know how to react to Martin's death. It had hit him hard, coming close after the deaths of two other long-time acquaintances from his years at work — both of them not much older than he was. Martin may have been a little younger. It was possible that this adventure to rescue a hearse could turn out to be something Martin might have enjoyed.

Bert Peterson and Herbie Brewer would lead the way in the blue Henry J that Arvo had fixed up for Peterson after finding it behind an abandoned sawmill off the Lower Road. This was Henry J Kaiser's short-lived experiment, a two-door car that looked, with its pointed nose, like a stunted shark. Or, some said, a two-seater plane without wings.

Arvo knew that if they were all to travel in the Henry J, he would have to sit in the back seat with his knees around his ears and his head bent forward against the slanted roof. Herbie was possessive of the front passenger seat just as he was possessive of just about everything else that was actually Peterson's, having so little he could actually call his own.

"I've been thinking," Arvo said, with one hand massaging the back of his neck. "This is a chance for me to take the Fargo for a spin, now I've got her back in running order."

Peterson shrugged. "No sense taking both. We'll just climb in with you."

Arvo put a hand on the roof of the Henry J and spoke to the ground. "It might be safer if you went ahead and kept me in your mirror. I don't want to get up into the hills and have 'er break down again."

Of course there was little chance of the Fargo breaking down. It was just that he didn't see any point in explaining the strategy he had in mind when he didn't know what sort of negotiating might be needed once they were up in the hills.

He took his portable license plate down off the wall of his workshop and hung it at the back end of the Fargo — a three-ton flat-bed truck a lumber company had left behind on its lot when it went out of business. Not worth the cost of repairs, they'd probably thought. Not worth the effort of finding someone to take it off their hands. If they'd poked around Arvo's place for a while they might have found all the parts it needed, and could even have flattered him into doing the job for the price of a month's groceries.

A scattering of white clouds had collected along the mountain peaks to the west, though the sky was otherwise clear and the late morning sun was still shining on the lower slopes — defining not only the curve of individual hills but the jagged patterns of still-standing timber as well.

The Henry J led the way inland, crossing the Creek on a wooden bridge, then passing one small fenced-in hobby farm after another, most of them cleared by families who'd arrived here just after the First World War. Some of their descendants still lived in houses built by their great-grandparents from a government-supplied pattern.

Younger family members had recently mowed and stacked the hay to dry in the fields. White-faced cattle cropped pasture grass or stared off into space, drool dangling from their chins. O'Hagen's dainty riding horses trotted along inside their fence, keeping pace with the Fargo as far as the end of the field.

Members of the Macken family, a rambunctious lot that never seemed to tire of one another's company, had built houses and developed hobby farms in every corner of the family's original acreage. Much of the original farm had been opened up for a gravel pit, which was no surprise when you remembered the old man complaining that he'd been unable to get a thing to grow on what he called "this goddam pile of rocks."

After crossing the Creek several times they passed through the site of what had been the Company town where Arvo had kept the trucks in good repair. All three rows of identical houses had been torn down or hauled away long ago, as had the Company office and the machine shop. Bert Peterson had been given the job of time-keeper in the office next door — after working for years on the booming grounds below town. They'd often eaten their lunches together on the roof, where they could enjoy the sun and the view out over the valley.

Martin had poked around in these remnants of a disappeared world now and then: chimney bricks and left-behind children's toys and chipped crockery that people had considered not worth the effort of packing up for the move. History had been important to him, especially local history, the story of the people he'd tried to represent in Ottawa. The folks who lived in this Company-owned cluster of buildings might have moved out to the highway or in to town but he found some sort of importance in the fact that this was where they had raised their children.

Alder had sprung up amongst the debris, but willows had grown along the river bank, as though to form a dense screen between this sad abandoned place and the logging-scarred blue mountains that reared up from beyond the river to their snowy peaks.

The pot-holed dusty road that for years had taken the loggers up into the hills now tunnelled beneath the new four-lane freeway and came out into a logged-off area blooming with tall pink foxgloves. They passed by an abandoned farm and a long stretch of second-growth Douglas fir, all precisely the same shape, the same eight-feet-tall, planted a few years ago as seedlings by a crew of university students.

The road that Peterson eventually turned onto was one that Arvo had not yet explored on his rescue missions. After no more than a few minutes of scanning the woods on either side, his practised eye had no difficulty spotting a red Toyota pickup parked beneath the giant cedars fewer than a hundred metres from the road. Someone hadn't cared enough to make sure the truck was abandoned where undergrowth would hide it from view. The lazy bugger had done Arvo a favour, however, since even if the Toyota was beyond repair it was bound to have any number of parts worth a return visit as soon as he'd got Martin's funeral out of the way.

They climbed a steep hill on a series of long rough switch-backs and eventually reached a plateau to level out through a shuddering stretch of washboard. From here he could look down upon a small gleaming lake like a woman's sapphire brooch dropped into a stand of spiky hemlock. The patchwork of small farms in Portuguese Creek spread out to the edge of the long blue stretch of the Strait with its scattered islands.

He hardly dared to hope that the hearse, once they'd found it, would be the one he remembered Old Man Birdsong driving at the head of a funeral parade — his pretty yellow-haired daughter beside him, sometimes even steering, though with her father's hand never far from the wheel. She had been in Arvo's class at school, had needed his help cleaning up her failed science experiments, and his advice for getting them right the next time she tried. She had been the school's prettiest girl — in his eyes at least — and of course she had known this about herself. She had probably known the effect she'd had on him even at that early age.

They travelled upwards along a side-hill where young firs were growing amongst the gigantic stumps left by the logged-off giants. When he'd first applied for a job in the woods, it was taken for granted by the bosses that he'd be a faller like most of the other Finns in the district, though he'd wanted only to be a mechanic. He'd had to set chokers for four or five years before they'd finally transferred him to the machine shop as Sparky Desmond's helper, keeping the steam locomotive in good repair, and then, once the loci and Sparky had both passed into history, servicing the large White and Kenworth trucks.

At the top of a long rough slope, they found themselves in a cleared space of raw stirred-up dirt, with a small unpainted plywood house at the far end. Peterson pulled over to one side and stopped, then oared his arm outside his window to encourage Arvo on past. It seemed they had arrived.

Arvo pulled up behind the Henry J and stopped, letting the Fargo motor tick over while he had a good look at what appeared to be someone's home. The house was roughly nailed with mismatched boards of various widths and thickness — some fir, some rough-sawn yellow cedar. Part of the roof was overlaid by a sheet of black plastic held in place by a heap of rocks at each corner. Whoever lived here could be squatters, or they could have a license for salvage. A half-ton Ford pickup without fenders or wheels rested on stacks of wood blocks, most of its yellow paint eaten up by rust. A dog house sat at a slant, a limp chain lying out across dirt as though a dog had taken a good hard run and broken free. A pair of speckled hens pecked at a scraggly patch of grass.

And, just as he had hoped, when he'd moved the Fargo slowly forward he could see the old hearse parked at an angle at the base of a clothesline pole off the far back corner of the house. It was almost certainly the one Joe Hudson had used to deliver his butchered meat after Thomas Birdsong had bought a newer model for his funerals. No one else had owned one of these, so far as he knew. A Cadillac — the *Cathedral Hearse*. He recognized the open-air driver's cab, the long hood and longer running board with the encased side-mounted spare wheel, the row of windows and elaborately carved frame of the carriage. As he drove slowly closer he could see that its lower half was caked with hardened mud.

This was disgusting: the mud, no garage to protect the hearse from weather, this isolated dusty location, and, worst of all the evidence that the hearse had been employed in some way for a private salvage operation, even for hauling poles down out of the bush.

He climbed down from the Fargo for a closer look, slowly circling the long black vehicle that made him think of a nineteenth-century stagecoach trying to convert itself into a modern limousine. Having no roof to protect it, the driver's seat was strewn with fallen twigs and rotting leaves, and had obviously suffered from weather. Aside from this and a shallow dent to the left rear corner, the hearse appeared to be in fairly good shape. He ran a hand down the long hood and the large chrome-plated headlamps, then twisted the cap off the radiator. The water was up. He raised the long engine cover to check the motor: it was clean, obviously cared-for, probably in good working order.

Since there was no question in his mind that this was the same hearse he'd tuned up for old man Hudson's meat deliveries, he already knew some things about it — that the body was designed by "Fletcher" for instance; that the synchro-mesh transmission allowed for three speeds forward. The clutch was a twin-disc version. For its time, it was definitely a luxury model. It still was, for that matter. A beauty.

He crouched to examine the tires. The rubber was firm, the tread on three of them worn but still safe enough, but the fourth — rear left — was dangerously close to bald.

Returning to the cab, he opened the backwards-opening half-door, brushed leaves and twigs from the seat, then slipped in behind the wheel. The engine turned over once, twice, a third time — then rumbled and ticked, sputtered a bit, and finally idled into a comfortable hum.

This was not just someone's tractor or Hudson's old butcher wagon; it was the hearse that Thomas Birdsong had driven at the head of any number of parades from church to cemetery through the city of Arvo's childhood. Before his family moved north to Portuguese Creek, he'd seen those funeral processions moving down the street — probably quite often, since he had such a vivid memory of Birdsong's daughter sitting where her father ought to be. She'd waved to those she passed by as though she believed herself to be driving a float in the First of July parade. Her father beamed with pride, or possibly with the pleasure of defying the police. But if the police had noticed this flouting of the law they'd done nothing about it. Maybe they were unwilling to interfere with a funeral. Even as a ten- or eleven- or twelve-year-old boy, he had been aware that he was seeing something astonishing, a vehicle more beautiful than any he'd seen before.

He was not aware of the woman until she was nearly upon him. "What do you think you're doing? Get away from there *you*!"

Arvo stepped onto the running board with both arms high, as he might if she'd confronted him with a gun. But he couldn't keep the grin from his face. He had found himself a beauty here, in need of very little attention. Martin would be pleased.

The woman stooped to take up a long slice of broken lumber off the ground and came at him as though ready to swat him with it. "Get down off of there right now!" Her large hips and powerful thighs were encased in faded jeans worn through at the knees. Her yellow woolly slippers were no strangers to this dirt.

"I meant no harm," he said. "Any damage I can see has been done already by someone else."

She came still closer and put a hand against the hood. "My boys don't like strangers poking around."

"I can understand that."

"So you can get back in your truck and leave."

Peterson and Herbie Brewer had got out of the Henry J and were now doing their own inspection of the hearse.

"You take good care of this vehicle?" Arvo asked. Still standing on the running board, he kept a hand on the steering wheel. "Somebody's kept her motor in pretty good shape, though that rear corner looks as though you might've backed into a tree."

"My boys depend on it," she admitted, nodding her head more times than was necessary. "It hauls the smaller logs, and sometimes drags the hand plough through my garden when I need it. And the harrows."

Herbie Brewer opened the door at the rear. "There's a sleeping bag in here," he said.

The woman seemed to find this an additional indignity. "You see the two-bit shack I got to live in? I got three sons, all big noisy louts.

Sometimes they snore so bad the windows rattle. A person can't *sleep*. You see a guest house anywhere, or even a tool shed? This has to be my bedroom now and then if I'm to get any rest at all." Perhaps sensing she had a good audience here, she allowed herself to grin. "I figure if I die in my sleep it'll be a convenience for the boys."

Herbie snickered. Peterson cleared his throat and turned away to examine the ground behind him. Arvo buttoned up the top button on his shirt and then unbuttoned it. It was not possible to know whether she was joking, though her scowl did seem to be daring them to laugh.

"It makes a pretty good tractor," she added. "If you came to make me an offer it better be a good one. The boys depend on this thing and would need to find another."

"Madam," Arvo said. "You and your sons have committed something like a sacrilege here! But we will forgive you if you'll let us borrow this hearse for a day or two."

"Can't," she said. "The boys'll kill me if they find her gone." She cocked her head to one side to add: "Especially since I know you're lying and won't never bring 'er back."

Peterson said, "We'll return it just as soon as we've done the best we can for a good friend of ours who died."

We will return it, Arvo did not say, but not to you or your sons. He was imagining the look on Myrtle Birdsong's face when she discovered he'd driven her father's hearse up to her door. "But in order to return it we have to borrow it first," he said. "And before we borrow it with the intention of returning it, we will need to see your ownership papers."

"Don't be a fool," she said. "We *found* this thing where somebody ditched it in the bush. There weren't no papers in it. We never take it near a public road."

"My friend Herbie here is good friends with the RCMP."

Though obviously a little startled by Arvo's way of putting it, Herbie Brewer grimly nodded his head. It was true that he spent a little time in the police station in town now and then, though only when he'd forgotten where he was supposed to meet up with Peterson for a ride home.

"Suppose we drive away right now and Herbie gets in touch with his pals and his pals are able to tell him who's the legal owner of this hearse. Unless you have a gun in your apron pocket and use it right now to shoot all three of us, I'll turn this machine around and we'll be on our way."

"You'll have to drive it over me first," the woman said. She moved in front of the hearse and spread her arms.

"It's a pleasure to see such determination," Arvo said. "But I'll tell you what we'll do." He stepped down and crossed the dirt to the Fargo and removed the portable license plate and carried it back through his own raised dust to the hearse and hung it off the door handle at the rear. "I have no intention of stealing the hearse, or even borrowing it. I came prepared to make a trade if I had to. I'll take this old hearse that was never meant for heavy labour off your hands in exchange for my three-ton Fargo in good working order — far better for the sort of work your sons are doing here. And, since you've obviously been getting away without a license or ownership papers up here in the bush, you'll be able to do the same with the Fargo. There's no sleeping compartment on the back but I'm sure your sons will be so pleased to see the trade you made they'll offer to build you one." He removed the sleeping bag and handed it to the woman.

Once he'd got into the hearse and started moving ahead, she lost interest in risking her life and stepped aside to shower him with curses.

Peterson waited until they'd got a hundred metres down the first slope to bring the Henry J to a stop, roll down his window, and wave for Arvo to pull up beside him. "You had that trade in mind from the start?"

Arvo grinned. "Did you think we were driving two vehicles all the way up here just to turn around and drive three vehicles back?"

"Sonofagun," Peterson said. Then he said, "Now that I seen that thing, I'm having second thoughts. It may be a little crazy to think you'll drive her all the way down to the city for Martin."

"She looks in pretty good shape to me," Arvo said. "I'll tune her up a bit before I go."

"And what if she breaks down on the road? What if the cops catch sight of you and decide to confiscate that hearse and throw you in the can?"

It was a legitimate concern, but Arvo chose to shrug it off. "So, it will be an adventure either way."

"It'll be an adventure once the undertakers in town get wind of what you're up to — horning in on their business. If you're stopped by the cops it will be Henderson or one of the others have put them up to it. They'll sue your skinny ass off."

Arvo narrowed his eyes. "Is this your way of saying you don't want to come along?"

"Sonofabitch." Peterson grinned. "You got any more surprises up your sleeve?"

"What I've got up my sleeve will have to stay up my sleeve for a while. Let's get moving. We'll need to stop somewhere to fill 'er up and give 'er a bit of a wash."

"Wash or no wash, we still don't know why that hospital should hand Martin over to us. I hope you've got *that* bit of information up your sleeve as well."

"I've got those papers Martin had me sign," Arvo said. "I just have to remember where I put them."

CHAPTER 3

⁕

FOR THE REST OF THAT afternoon he kept the doors to his work-shop closed and barred. If anyone were to see him tinkering with a vintage hearse, phones would soon be ringing all over the district. Matt Foreman would cross the road to bombard him with questions he was not prepared to answer. *Was he sure it was legal to be doing this? Who did he think would want this old thing once he had it back in good running order?* Before long, half the district would be standing in his doorway to watch, everyone with an opinion.

He wasn't about to forget the way they'd reacted when he'd been spotted hauling in an orange Renault he'd found behind Cougar Lake. No one could recall ever having seen a Renault before, orange or otherwise. Everyone wanted to have a look, everyone wanted to sit behind the wheel and discover what it felt like to drive a French automobile. A French *voiture*! Minnie Lewis swore she could smell Parisian perfume in the upholstery, though Arvo's nose could recognize only mould. Brian Lundy closed his eyes and imagined, aloud, that he was cruising down the Champs Elysées, circling the Arc de Triomphe. But Arvo began to suspect the car might have been offended by this excessive attention, since no matter how much he tinkered, the damn thing rabbit-hopped across intersections as though it were trying to throw him through the windshield.

When he'd realized there was no hope the others would allow him to establish a private relationship with the unruly foreign car, he removed all re-usable parts and stored them in the loft on the slim chance that another needy Renault might show up during his lifetime. The chassis quickly disappeared beneath the weeds and vines behind his house.

It was possible that someone had seen him drive the Cathedral hearse onto his property, but they would have to be content with imagining what he was up to. The workshop's windows were too high for anyone to see without going to the trouble of bringing an extension ladder.

Not even Peterson and Herbie Brewer were welcome to watch. Once the hearse was safely inside his shop, he'd suggested they leave. "I never worked on a hearse before. I don't want to think about anything else."

"You forget who found this thing?" Herbie said.

"He knows who found her," Peterson said. "He knows we showed him the way to get to her, too, so he could bring her back and act like he found her himself."

"Dammit," Arvo said. "I'd like to get this out on the road first thing tomorrow. You think Martin can wait much longer?"

Peterson was not happy about this, but Herbie reminded him that they'd promised Cynthia they would stop by to fix the catch on her gate. "She's scared Glover's bull will get into her yard and ambush her when she goes out to pull her carrots."

It wasn't easy for Arvo to imagine a bull fierce enough to scare Cynthia Howard. She might be small — "wiry" was the word she used for herself — but she could be as "fierce" as any bull if she needed to be. He'd been told that even the tallest toughest student would cower when she gave them a certain side-long look, though he had never seen this for himself.

As soon as he'd barred the pair of doors, and drawn the bolt across the inset door as well, he started up the hearse in order to listen closely to its engine. Only the slightest adjustment was needed in order to get it idling as smoothly as he knew it should. "She's sounding hopeful," he said. He turned the engine off and leaned in to test the fan belt with his fingers. Still strong enough. "We'll soon be on our way, Martin, though I don't suppose you're any more interested in motors now than when you were alive."

The shed was narrower than his house but high enough for spare parts to be stored in the loft. The corrugated metal roof was laid over ten-inch beams that rested on rows of twelve-inch posts. His tools — hacksaw, pipe cutter, pliers, grease gun, socket wrench, grease gun — hung on the wall above his workbench, which ran the full length of one wall, with a powerful vise-grip mounted at one end and a coffee maker at the other, beneath a coloured magazine photo of Elizabeth Taylor in her Cleopatra costume. Sunlight came in through the row of small windows just below the roof-line.

Beside the coffee maker and a goose-neck lamp was a kitchen chair where he could sit to read his mechanics magazines for a break without having to clean himself up and return to the house. Cans of motor oil and rolls of paper towelling sat next to the tower of James

Lee Burke crime novels, most of them set in New Orleans. If the stories were to be believed, every minute he'd wandered those streets his innocent tourist life had been in danger — from gunshots, speeding cars, escaped convicts, vicious drug runners, and carloads of demented killers. It was a miracle he'd survived.

As he worked, he was aware of traffic racing by on the Old Highway. Occasionally an automobile turned onto the side road to pass by in front of his workshop. Tires on pavement hummed today, though sometimes after a light rain they could sound like adhesive bandages being ripped from skin. Whenever someone turned too wide, tires crackled in shoulder gravel.

He held the dipstick high. Oil was clean and shiny to the "full" line. That woman's sons had taken pretty good care of the hearse, even while treating it like some sort of tractor. He had good reason to believe that by the time the sun had started to rise above the firs tomorrow he'd have her ready for the journey south.

Until the age of thirteen, when his parents moved up here to Portuguese Creek, he had lived in the city where Martin Glass had died in hospital and where Charlie Birdsong had been the undertaker who'd owned this hearse — also the father of a pretty blonde-haired daughter. Of course it had been a surprise the first time he'd seen a classmate behind the wheel at the head of a funeral procession.

In order not to lose sight of her then, he had walked beside the hearse up the main street, across an intersection and the railroad tracks and the river bridge, and then through the downtown area to the stone-pillared entrance to the grassy cemetery. Perhaps her father had installed a governor, maybe he'd kept his own foot on the gas pedal, since the hearse, so far as Arvo could tell, had maintained precisely the same speed throughout the entire route.

Though he had been aware of her presence every day in the Grade Five classroom, it wasn't until he'd seen her driving her father's hearse — her golden curls and pretty face a contrast to all that sober black — that he'd become fascinated with this girl. Of course he hadn't suspected then that he would be thinking of her for much of the rest of his life.

Throughout the years that followed, he had tried to forget her — and of course it was ridiculous, an adult man still captivated by a childhood memory. Even during his travels he'd continued to wonder what had become of Myrtle Birdsong. They might very well have come upon one another in Oslo, say, or Baton Rouge. He still subscribed to the city newspaper and had now and then come across her name. Recently, her photo had been alongside an account of the opening of a new theatre named for her father, who had apparently been a generous supporter of local drama clubs.

So she was still alive and living in the city of his birth.

Though he was not sure he had the courage to return her father's hearse to Myrtle himself — after all, he couldn't know for sure that she would welcome it — this was no reason to turn down a chance to get this beautiful vehicle back in good running order for Martin's funeral. Once he'd accomplished that much, he might feel brave enough to deliver it to its original owner's daughter — though of course he had serious doubts.

He could not be slow about it. Martin Glass's death was a reminder that your life could go flying by more quickly than you'd ever imagined. Martin had often talked of his plan to look up his son in Saskatchewan one day and — despite the son's politics, his rejection of his father, his eccentric lifestyle in some remote northern town — try to establish some sort of peaceful relationship. But he had put off making the journey until "another day." He could not have imagined his life could run out so soon.

Arvo flushed out the radiator and filled it with water from his well. He tested the hoses — brittle but still secure. He checked the wheel nuts — all tight. This was important, since he could hardly avoid thinking of the jeep he'd rescued from a long-abandoned army training camp in the mountains. Because he hadn't thought to check the wheel nuts, the back left-side wheel detached itself while he was driving down the highway and travelled independently past him on a long downhill slope. Only when the wheel had gone spinning off ahead and veered across the oncoming traffic to leap into the road-side weeds did the back corner of the jeep drop to the pavement and bring the whole business squealing to a halt. Remembering this, he could break out in a sweat even now.

He tried to keep at bay the doubts that Peterson had raised — the possibility of a breakdown far from home, or interference by police. It was also possible they could get all the way to the city only to find that Myrtle wasn't at home. Travelling maybe. And of course there was also the possibility that even if she were at home she could turn him away — not wanting a reminder of her father or of the husband who'd worked for her father, or anything at all that reminded her of her childhood.

She had sat directly in front of him in Grades Six and Seven, her long curls occasionally brushing his desk, and often turned to ask him to explain what the teacher was talking about. She had been Snow White in the school play while he was only a woodcutter — but this meant it was sometimes necessary for her to walk home with him to practise their lines in his mother's kitchen. She had barely noticed his help with her failed science experiments or with anything else, and he had not found the nerve to tell her how he felt, knowing they were both too young for such nonsense.

He'd lived long enough in the city to see her reach adolescence sooner than any other girl her age. Even at thirteen she caused men to turn and watch her walk down the street.

Several years after his family had moved north, he'd learned that

Myrtle had married a middle-aged Hungarian her father had brought to this country to be his assistant. No doubt she'd married him so she would never have to leave her father's side. Much later still, he'd heard that the husband had been an unsatisfactory assistant and had returned to Hungary, though not until after he'd done a good deal of damage to the business.

Myrtle had not abandoned her father. He had seen her name several times in the arts-and-society pages of the city paper. Apparently she was either a divorced woman or a widow, and might now be running her father's business herself or, more likely, living in some sort of luxury, having sold the business to someone else.

He knew it was unrealistic to imagine a reunion. Yet trying to forget her had led him into nothing but trouble. He had even, once, considered a mail-order sort of bride. He'd known that Johnnie Banner, who for a while had been his assistant in the Company machine shop, was happily married to the widowed school teacher who'd responded to his ad in the Winnipeg Free Press.

It had taken him three months of writing and throwing away his own advertisement for "meeting a middle-aged woman interested in a visit to the West Coast with other possibilities to follow" but before he had sent his advertisement off, he'd come across a notice in the Vancouver Sun, where a "woman of Finnish background living in the Port Arthur area of Thunder Bay" was looking for a cousin who had disappeared out west. Arvo had recognized the name of a long-ago fellow worker in the logging camps and wrote to tell her of his death. What had been an exchange of brief notes — friendly but not *too* friendly, he'd thought — had apparently seemed, to her, something like a marriage proposal.

One afternoon, without warning, she had stepped down off the bus in front of the Store — a large woman, with three grey suitcases and a teenaged son who had not been mentioned in the letters. Ritva Pekkanen and Toivo. The mother was determined on a trial period "to see if we're suited to one another." The son was determined not to return to Thunder Bay, where "the stupid cops like to pick on me."

So he now had the unforgettable memory of this woman and her lunk-head son moving into his house and making a nervous wreck of him. By the time he'd got them back on a bus, three months had gone by in which he'd paid Toivo's bail three times and failed to stave off Ritva Pekkenen's efforts to move most of his mother's Helsinki knick-knacks to the basement in exchange for junk she'd found in local yard sales. They would be "house mates for now, nothing more," she'd said, and he was not about to argue. Yet she'd behaved as though his home were hers. She invited neighbours in for tea in the afternoons — women who had not been inside the house since the death of Arvo's mother. She'd decided what groceries Arvo must buy. She'd complained when Arvo spent too much time in his work-shop, and tried hard to train him to spend his evenings reading the paper and "keeping company with Toivo and myself," instead of ducking back out to his "greasy engines and such."

He'd been ashamed of himself even then for putting up with this, but he'd suspected it was his own fault. It was his punishment for not investigating this woman somehow, before writing to her. But how could he have known she would show up without so much as a phone conversation?

For his daily before-dinner sauna he'd locked the door from the inside for fear she would surprise him one day by entering, stripping off, and joining him on the upper bench, then later use this as an ex-cuse for insisting upon a trip to a justice of the peace. While he sat sweating on the upper bench he tried to recall what he'd imagined when he'd written that letter.

Wrenches and screwdrivers disappeared from his workshop and reappeared on the walls of the pawnshop in town. He found himself paying to rescue an electric drill that he'd only recently paid for in a hardware store. The boy did not bother denying that he'd had something to do with this. When the police occasionally kept him overnight after finding him drunk and pestering folks on the main street of town, they apologized to Arvo for not having the legal right to keep him longer. "Maybe if you let him wreck your truck or burn your sauna down we could put him away for a while."

But Toivo stole only items you didn't remember you had until you went to use them.

On evenings when he wasn't out getting himself into trouble, he sprawled across the chesterfield, with his huge feet up on the arm, watching something his mother had chosen for him to watch on television. He had no homework to do since he'd refused to go anywhere near the local school so long as his mother was uncertain how long they'd be staying on.

Then one night the boy had trouble finding the doorknob — or maybe even the door — in order to let himself into the house. He'd tossed stones at his mother's window to get her up from her bed to let him in, but before she'd got to the door a stone had broken through the glass and fallen against a decorative crystal bowl of his mother's, causing a visible crack to travel around its waist.

Although the bowl was only one of several, and the fissure did not cause the bowl to fall in pieces, Arvo rushed out of his bedroom wearing only the sagging bottoms of his striped pyjamas and clasped both hands around the boy's neck. He uttered several words he hadn't used since he'd been a teen himself. The boy gurgled. The mother screamed. The boy's eyes grew large. The mother, cursing, slapped at Arvo from every side, but the hands would not let go.

And did not let go until the eyes rolled up and the body went limp.

"You beast!" screamed the woman from Thunder Bay. "You've killed him!"

But the boy was still alive enough to pack their belongings into the grey suitcases and carry one of them out to the bus stop, where he waited for Arvo to do whatever he could to get his mother outside and onto the bus for her journey home.

Good-bye!

Arvo washed the dried mud from the hearse's flank and the dust from the windows — pure pleasure. There wasn't much he could do about the fine hair-line crack in a corner of one panel of glass, but he could make sure all the windows were spotless.

He paused to admire the hearse while eating a slice of the date loaf Cynthia had left for him yesterday. She seemed to have got into the habit of bringing some of her baking with her now and then, though he was not to let the others know. In return, he sometimes gave her a loaf of his *pulla*, the sweet bread he'd baked from his mother's recipe.

When he'd got down into the pit and looked up at the hearse's undercarriage, he could see that all moveable parts could do with a shot of grease. But first he wiped everything down to get rid of the accumulated dirt — to be expected in the circumstances.

On his way through town tomorrow he would stop at Henderson's Funeral Home to pick up a casket suitable for a friend who happened to be a long-forgotten one-term member of Her Majesty's Loyal Opposition. Martin was one of those former public officials whose obituary must have been a surprise to people who'd thought he'd died long years ago. The people of Portuguese Creek may have been the only ones aware of the quiet retirement life of Martin Glass, down at the water's edge.

Once he was satisfied with the sound of the engine, he went inside the house just long enough to telephone the hospital, identify himself again as Martin Glass's executor, and let those in charge of bodies know that he would be there to pick up Martin tomorrow on behalf of the Henderson Funeral Home, probably late afternoon, in order to bring him home for burial. When he returned to the shed he carried a wool blanket his mother had brought with her from Finland, draped it over the weather-damaged seat and tucked it in where he could. Now a perfect row of little Suomi birches marched from one end of the bench to the other.

Of course this hearse must not be allowed out on the road again without receiving a good wash and a new coat of wax, a task that kept him occupied for more than an hour. He wiped again over the head lamps and the large panels of glass, polished the chrome handles, and then washed out the interior of the chamber where a casket, and eventually Martin, would rest.

For some time he'd been aware of the muffled sound of lowered voices outside the shed but had thought nothing of it. People sometimes chatted as they walked away from the Store. But now there was an impatient banging on the inset door, an attempt to push it open.

"Arvo? You in there?"

It was Matt Foreman's voice. Running the Store and post office made him think he had the right to know everyone's business. It was as though he wanted you to know he could read your mail if he wanted to but had generously chosen not to — so the least you could do in return was to tell him more of your business than you'd tell anyone else.

"Who is it?"

"It's Matt."

"Who?"

Why let him think he sprang immediately to mind? There were

other Matts in the world. After owning the store for only four or five years he was still a newcomer here.

"It's Matthew Foreman."

"Sorry Matt. I guess I'd never heard you shouting through a locked solid-oak door before. What do you want?"

"Just checking. We heard you moving around in there but it's not like you to work with the door closed and locked."

"The 'closed' is meant to be a hint. The 'locked' is for them that don't know how to take a hint."

"We just want to make sure you're okay. Maggie said you were feeling a little dizzy when she saw you Monday."

"I always feel a little dizzy on Mondays. The sound of everyone racing off to work on Monday mornings makes my head spin."

"I hope you don't start up any motors with the doors closed." There was a sort of embarrassed chuckle in his voice. "We don't want you asphyxiating yourself."

"What *do* you want, Matt? I'm working on something that could ruin any number of lives if I don't get 'er right. And the clock is ticking away while I stand here shouting at you."

All of this was true, though he hadn't thought of putting it quite that way until now. His own future, Martin's future, perhaps even Myrtle Birdsong's future depended upon his making sure this hearse was in top shape before he set out tomorrow morning for the city.

"I was joking, Arvo. We know you're a man of good sense. It's just that I've got someone here who wants to have a word. If you won't let us in, maybe you'll come out. It won't take more than a few minutes."

"This *someone* doesn't have a name?"

"Ms., uh, Edwards — from a home-and-family magazine? Happened to be in the Store when she heard someone wondering what you were up to. Alice Redmond said she could swear she seen the tail end of a hearse disappearing into your shop a few hours ago."

"You sure she didn't say 'tail end of a horse?'"

"If you had a horse in there we'd smell it even through your god-damn three-inch doors. I don't smell anything but grease and oil the same as always. This lady says she only wants a few minutes of your time. It won't take her any longer than that to see if you're a story worth her writing up. Might even take your picture."

"Tell her if she comes back around noon tomorrow she might get a story if she can find me. Right now I'm too busy to talk to her or anyone else."

There was some whispering and muttering outside the doors before Foreman said, "We're going. Ms. Edwards may come back tomorrow or she may not. You could have missed your chance to see your picture in a magazine."

"I've lived for three-quarters of a century without seeing my picture in a magazine. I guess I can manage to live a little longer without."

"Suit yourself," Foreman said, making it sound like some kind of warning. Footsteps crunched in gravel, moving away.

But then returned. "My father owned a pair of Clydesdales," Matt Foreman's voice said. "If you had a horse in there I would've smelled the sonofabitch. I think you've got a hearse in there. If Mizz Edwards decides you're doing something illegal you can be sure she'll hound you till she's found the truth."

"I didn't hear a word you said, Matt," Arvo said, turning away. "I'm too busy to pay attention to gossip."

Whether or not this Ms. Edwards came back, it was important to get this Cadillac out on the road and heading south as early as possible tomorrow, certainly before Matthew Foreman was awake and spying out his side window.

Naturally he would not let Bert Peterson or Herbie Brewer know that he had more than one reason for making this journey. He would rather be doing this alone but knew it wasn't possible. Peterson would be furious, Herbie disappointed. You don't allow your friends to lead you to a great opportunity and then leave them behind while you enjoy the rewards in secret.

This didn't mean that if he happened to wake up early he would sit around and wait for them to show up. Nor did it mean that if they did show up in time he would stop for any distractions that intrigued them, or make side-trips for some errand they wanted to run. They would be in Peterson's Henry J and could do whatever they pleased. He would simply keep on moving steadily down the highway in the direction of Martin's hospital morgue and, maybe, to Myrtle Bird-song's home in the city of his childhood years.

But before doing anything more, he would phone David Henderson to let him know that Martin had made his old friend Arvo his executor, and that Arvo was about to go down to rescue Martin from the city. If Henderson was interested in selling him a coffin today on their way through town, and later conducting some sort of funeral for their former Member of Parliament, and even making temporary use of a vintage Cadillac hearse for the occasion, maybe he would also be interested in filling out the proper paperwork requiring the hospital to hand the body over to Arvo as a temporary representative of his company.

CHAPTER 4

THIS TIME IT WAS Peterson hammering on the door. "I been thinking about Martin's boy. Shouldn't we be letting him know about the funeral?"

Martin's *boy* had to be fifty years old by now, a successful business-man somewhere east of the Rockies — or so they'd been told.

Arvo opened the inset door just wide enough for Peterson to slip through, then closed it and slid the bolt across. "He wouldn't visit his ol' man while he was alive, so why would he care about his funeral?"

"Well, he's bound to show up some time — to claim the house and all that waterfront property. He could be pissed we didn't let him know."

Arvo used the rag in his hand to erase his own fingerprints from the left-side headlamp. "Martin's lawyer will look after that."

Peterson waggled his shoulders, shaking off a topic that had probably been nothing more than an excuse to stop by. He grinned, eager to be in on things. "So — you got 'er ready yet?"

Arvo led him around to the far side of the hearse. "We should be able to head out early tomorrow morning, but there's still something I don't much like. Have a look at this rear tire."

"Still as bald as it was last time I looked." Peterson crouched to run his fingertips over the tread. "You think she's dangerous?"

"Well, tell me how you think we'll like hearing the hiss of it going flat when we're halfway home with Martin in the back and nowhere near a town."

Peterson grunted from the effort of getting himself upright.

"But the only place I can think of finding a good match to the others is out in Billy-boy Harrison's pasture."

"Ha!" Peterson said — not exactly a laugh. "You'll need an extension ladder then." Billy stacked old tires in tall black pillars out in his field. "Anyway, Billy won't be home. This is Arts and Crafts Day in Portuguese Creek." He said this with a bit of a sneer, while making quotation marks in the air with his fingers. "He'll be up at the hall, trying to sell his so-called art. Which you couldn't pay me to hang in my *barn*."

Billy-boy Harrison was one of the dozen or so Americans who'd shown up in Portuguese Creek during the Vietnam War — young men who'd chosen to live in this foreign country rather than let themselves be sent to die in another, or to sit in prison at home. Billy-boy had bought the old Houston dairy farm, as well as Wally Houston's herd of Jerseys, claiming his grandfather had a dairy herd in South Carolina. When he wasn't milking cows or delivering the milk, he fashioned "art works" out of junk he'd picked up at yard sales around the district.

When Arvo pulled in beside the community hall a half-mile north of the Store, several cars were parked in front of the big unpainted hip-roofed building, others in the gravel beside the road. Albert Taylor and Willie Ford leaned against the railing at the foot of the steps, sucking on their thin, flat, home-rolled cigarettes and deep in serious talk. Willie nodded to Arvo. Taylor raised a finger salute to the beak of his cap.

Inside, too many conversations were happening at once, most of them at the plywood folding tables to one end of the hall where you could buy coffee and doughnuts or a slice of blackberry pie. Harvey Foster raised a hand to greet Arvo without pausing in his grim-faced explanation of something aimed at Beryl Woods, who leaned back in her chair and seized Arvo's pant leg as he was about to pass. "Come here a minute!" When he crouched beside her, she lowered her voice to a growl. "When're you gonna have that pickup ready for my niece? Every time I go by your place I see 'er still parked in the weeds. Have you even bloody started?"

Although he was face-to-face with Beryl Woods, he avoided looking into her eyes, which were imperfectly aligned. "There's no use even starting till I've found a replacement for that cracked gear box."

"Have you *looked*?"

"I warned you, Beryl." Speaking to Beryl Woods usually required some care. She did not respond well to evasions. "Ford pickups just aren't showing up in the bush, or even the junkyards. I should've kept that little black Hillman for your niece."

"Bah!" Beryl Woods released him with a gesture that clearly said *Get away from me, you!*"

A series of tables had been set up down the length of the back wall, each with a local artist or artisan standing behind it — or, he supposed, a friend — ready to sell the wares displayed on the tables or hung on the wall at their backs. Knitted sweaters were taped, spread-eagled, to the plywood. Wood toys were lined up on home-made shelves. Walter Percy had brought his daughter with him this time, in case she attracted more interest in his walnut salt and pepper shakers — which wasn't likely so long as she kept that resentful expression on her face.

Billy-boy Harrison's table was between Percy's wooden toys and Maggie Reynolds' hooked rugs. Billy stood at attention, his fingers combing down through his patchy beard. On the wall behind him he'd hung half a dozen box-framed plywood squares, each filled with a variety of glued-together junk. One was crammed with broken crockery fitted together like a jig-saw puzzle, another with an assortment of small plumbing items: washers, a spindle top from a tap, an elbow coupling, a rubber bathtub plug with dangling chain, a T-junction joint.

"Looking for something, Mr. Saarikoski?"

"I am, Billy, yes."

He was tempted to accuse Billy of wasting perfectly good parts that someone could have used for a better purpose, but at least he hadn't sent them to the dump.

"You see anything you lack?"

Had he said "lack" or "like?" Arvo couldn't tell. If you'd forgotten that Billy-boy was from the Deep South, his slow accented drawl was a surprise. Some claimed he put it on, but Arvo suspected that Billy was too open-hearted to be skilled at deliberate falsity. "You're lookin' at my *Open Sesame* there. Those handles represent the opportunities that await us if we just open ourselves to the world."

"Is that so?" As far as Arvo knew, Billy-boy Harrison had never opened himself to the world beyond finding the fastest route between South Carolina and the Canadian border. "What I'm looking for today doesn't hang on walls. I need a tire."

Billy-boy's interest perked up. "Well, I have an abundance of those at home."

"I know that, Billy. I've seen them from the road. You stack up many more of those towers you'll have to apply for a building permit."

Billy-boy seemed pleased to hear this. "I don't suppose any old tire will do."

"I don't suppose it will." Arvo removed the note from his pocket and consulted his scribble. "I'm looking for a Series 353. Pretty rare." He read directly from the paper. "Seven, dot, zero, zero, dash, A. This is a 19-inch tire."

"Well, that's pretty darn specific. I'll have to check my records for one of those."

"I'd like some decent tread on it. And I'd rather you didn't take much time looking."

"What do you call decent tread?"

"You can start with *not bald* and work up from there." Arvo laughed to hear himself say this.

But Billy raised his eyebrows. "Well sir, I figure if you get much tread at all you'll be lucky."

"All I need right now is one that'll run a couple hundred k without a flat. You think you can find me that while I'm minding your stall?"

"I keep a record. I know where every tire is at. I like to keep them together with their own kind, if you know what I mean."

"I know what you mean, Billy. No man from South Carolina wants his Firestones mingling with his Goodyears."

"Ha ha. Go help yourself to a coffee. Whitey Burke stands in for me when I need a break."

Billy-boy Harrison slapped a soiled ball cap on his head and worked his way through the tables of coffee drinkers, pausing just long enough to say something to wild-haired Whitey Burke, and then left the hall tossing his keys in the palm of one hand.

Arvo was not much interested in the variety of home-made wares for sale — baked goods, knitted items, sewn aprons, preserves. He talked for a while with Kevin Williams, who was carving a small figure out of a block of yellow cedar — probably another owl to stand amongst the half dozen already lined up on a shelf with his miniature pigs and donkeys. Kevin reported that his mother's fourth marriage was turning out better than the earlier matches, possibly because this husband had no family to interfere. "I had my hopes pinned on *you* for a while there, Arvo, before this fellow showed up. You could have been my step-dad by now! She'd told me this time she'd decided to marry a Finn."

"Did she give a reason?"

"Well . . ." Kevin shrugged. "I suppose any old Finn would do. She'd got it into her head that any Finn that isn't a total drunk is hard-working, generous, and faithful — a sort of saint. For a while there I thought she was after you when she nearly drove me crazy asking the names for parts of a car. But then this other fellow showed up."

Maybe she *had* been after him, for a while. This would explain why Marketta Williams — whenever they'd been in the Store at the same time — had pestered him with so many questions about what to look for when you were in the market for a new car. She was an attractive woman, a little flirtatious; she had a habit of putting a hand on your arm while she talked to you. Her interest in cars had eventually given him the courage to invite her to a movie in town. Four different movies, four Saturdays in a row — he could recall their titles if he had to. They'd stopped at the Arbutus Hotel each time for a

45

drink, and twice she'd invited him in to her house afterwards. But then she'd met "this other fellow" somewhere and, he imagined, had been swept right off her feet.

"This guy is a Swede," Kevin said. "I guess she looked at a map and decided a Swede must be nearly the same as a Finn! Close call, eh? You should be relieved. My mother has a habit of outliving her husbands."

Arvo left Kevin Williams gouging his little owl out of the block of yellow cedar, then passed by several home-made quilts to examine the prizes to be won in the draw: a weekend in Seattle or a collection of Marjorie McGowan's jams. He helped himself to a coffee and took it to a table where Jenny Banks sat alone. He would drink the coffee and then go home to wait for Billy there.

"A good thing Picasso never glued car parts to his pictures," Earl Boyd said, bringing his own mug of coffee to the table. "I seen you eyeing Billy-boy's works of art. With you around, Picasso would never've got his painting to the galleries before you found some reason to hijack them for your workshop! The man would be a pauper to this day."

"Picasso's dead." Jenny Banks said this across the top of her mug.

"So he'd be in a pauper's grave," Earl said. "Arvo's fault."

Arvo looked down at his own two open hands. "I wasn't after Billy's *art*."

"Help yourself to one of these buns," Jenny said, holding out a paper bag to Arvo. "You could be waiting awhile. Sometimes Billy has a little trouble living up to his promises. He told his mother he'd be back in South Carolina for her birthday but he hasn't got around to it yet. After forty years. You willing to wait that long for Billy-boy's tire?"

"I'm surprised you haven't had a visit from the Big Car Manufacturers," Earl said, directing an obvious wink at the others. "Every wreck you bring back to life is another new car they don't get to sell. You're undermining the economy of Japan and the US, both. Ontario too."

Arvo had heard this before. It was a harmless sort of joking, though you sensed a hint of something serious beneath it when it came from Earl Boyd.

He supposed he was a bit of a mystery to some. Few in Portuguese Creek were allowed to remain mysteries for long — it wasn't neighbourly. Still, though he minded his own business, he tried to be friendly to all. Of course they probably believed that a man with his head under a raised engine hood had little real life of his own.

Rick Morrison walked his chair over from a neighbouring table and swung it around to face them. "Never mind the Big Car Manufacturers — what about the sales staff on our own car lots? Lowest number of sales gets his walking papers. You like putting people out of work?"

"Arvo's a bit of an anarchist at heart." Jenny said this as though she rather hoped it was true. Her father had been an outspoken member of the IWW when Arvo and Jenny were in elementary school together. At the time, Arvo had had only the vaguest idea of what the IWW was — something foreign in origin, frowned-upon, dangerous, vaguely communist. Jenny had come to school in faded cut-down cotton dresses. No socks in her shoes. Her father had been sent to jail for a while. She'd married young — a distant cousin in Alberta — but had come home a widow, and soon afterwards married Jerry Banks, the owner of the largest lumber company in town. She was a widow now again, living alone in a mansion she and Banks had built where her parents' shack once stood. Recently she'd been elected president of the Community Association.

By the time Arvo had finished a second coffee, Billy-boy Harrison had returned. "Got 'er!" he said. "Easy!" He threw his arms out wide, waiting to be welcomed with praise and applause.

Earl Boyd applauded, slowly, with his big hands. Sarcastically, it seemed to Arvo.

"Your tire's outside," Billy-boy said. "I don't know how much tread there is but you can see there's some — which is more than I can say for most of the others."

"What's this for?" Alec Morrison turned to ask Arvo.

"Finding the tire was easier than I thought," Billy-boy said. "So I spent a couple of minutes on the internet. I was curious to see what sort of vehicle it's for."

"And?" Earl said.

"Billy knows all business between us is confidential," Arvo said.

Billy-boy shrugged. "Don't worry. It's nobody else's business how much a person pays. And it's nobody else's business if that tire is meant for a logging truck, a Smart Car, or a big old Cadillac."

"You're finding abandoned logging trucks now?" Alex Morrison scowled at Arvo. "How the hell would you get a logging truck down out of the woods without anyone knowing?"

"Someone would have noticed," Beryl Wood said. "The police are probably at your place this minute. Don't expect us to vouch for you. We don't know what you do when you're alone."

"Yes, we do," said Earl. "He spends it tinkering like a kid with his Meccano set."

"Do they still make Meccano sets?" Beryl asked. "They have Lego now."

"It probably isn't a logging truck," Alex Morrison said.

"Well, it can't be a Cadillac," Beryl said. "Who would ditch a Cadillac out in the bush? Anyone who owns a Cadillac would trade it in for a new one — or maybe an Audi."

"I don't know if they even *make* Cadillacs any more," Earl said. "Maybe they're like Meccano sets, replaced by plastic Lego cars from Denmark."

CHAPTER 5

❧

HE TURNED ONE WAY and then, within minutes, the other. The blankets made him too warm, and yet he had never been able to sleep without a cover. It was impossible to relax, knowing that the Cathedral hearse sat unguarded in his workshop while Matt Foreman across the road was probably awake and wondering how he could discover what his neighbour was hiding. No doubt he was waiting until he could be confident Arvo was asleep before sneaking over to pry open the doors. This would require no more than a half-decent crowbar.

Of course people here did not act like that. And anyway, a crowbar would cause nails to squeal loud enough to wake any number of households.

Maybe he should just take his blankets out and curl up on the driver's seat of the hearse.

Not a good idea, somehow, to fall asleep in a hearse. Foreman and his crowbar would find him stiff and cold. He could imagine the local newspaper: *Man Dies In Hearse: friends claim he liked to make things easy for others*.

A sound from outside was probably a raccoon testing a garbage can lid, but just in case it was Foreman — or maybe Eleanor Robinson, a woman who seemed to think she had the right to know everyone's business — he sat up and parted the curtains to check.

But he could see no unfamiliar shapes out there. No movement.

With his head on the pillow again, he remembered that Peter Sleggart had once admitted that he had a sleepwalking habit, and had wakened one night to find himself in Margaret Robinson's bed. "What are you doing in my bed?" he was supposed to have said, indignantly, when he recognized Margaret asleep beside him. Margaret had laughed about it later, but her husband, once he'd returned from a business trip, was not amused. Sleggart could possibly use this same explanation if he were intercepted while leaning an extension ladder against the window wall of the workshop. "In my dream I decided to go up and clean out your eaves."

Eventually he got up out of bed, put a mackinaw over his pyjamas, and went outside with a flashlight to check that the hearse was still where he'd left it.

Of course he knew he could be about to make a fool of himself, expecting Myrtle Birdsong to be grateful that he had rescued her father's hearse. But it was important he find out at last whether he ought to have forgotten her long ago. How much had he missed in life by holding onto an adolescent crush?

He was still awake at 4:00 a.m.

Portuguese Creek was populated with any number of people who were used to having their curiosity satisfied by others willing to tell them all of their business. Arvo's locked doors could be seen as a challenge, even an insult. There was bound to be someone who felt it his duty to satisfy everyone's curiosity while teaching Arvo Saarikoski a lesson.

At 4:30, he decided that he was being childish to worry about a possible disappointment at the Birdsong doorstep, and a fool to think that others cared enough to see what was in his workshop to break in during the night. He checked that the alarm he'd set for 6:30 hadn't changed its mind, and lowered his head to the pillow.

In sleep he revisited the city he hadn't seen in forty years. In Helsinki's harbour market, people turned from their buying and selling to claim him enthusiastically as one of their own. But before taking him home for *kahvi* and *jalkiruokia* they insisted he help them dredge up from the harbour floor the multitude of trucks and cars that had been driven off the pier by drunks and fools. But his protests were ignored, and he soon found himself drifting through a watery graveyard of vehicles with unfamiliar shapes, designed no doubt by Russians or Swedes. When he recognized Herbie, Bert Peterson, and Cynthia behind the windshield glass of a rusty Saab, his own horrified shout jolted him out of sleep.

Sitting up, with blankets spilled out around him onto the carpeted floor, he discovered he was alive and still breathing air. By pushing aside the window curtain he could see in the weak morning light the rough unpainted wall of his workshop, and, on the far side of the road, the dark side-window of the General Store.

Even so, something disagreeable was taking its time to rise from the dark sea of his memory. News of something cruel had recently arrived.

Martin Glass had died.

Martin had died and Arvo was about to bring him home.

By the time he'd eaten a quick breakfast at his kitchen table, dressed in his black denim jeans and a white washed-and-ironed shirt, and had gone outside to unlock the workshop, the Henry J had crossed the Old Highway from Stevenson Road and was pulling up in front of the double doors, a plywood sign with large red letters fastened to the front bumper:

!!SLOW HEARSE FOLLOWING!!

Peterson rolled down his window to explain in a stage whisper. "Herbie stayed up half the night to make it."

Grinning, Herbie Brewer stepped out of the Henry J and held up a second sign. "This one's for the back of the hearse."

SORRY

WE'RE GOING

AS FAST AS WE CAN

Otherwise, Peterson said, they'd have to put up with a whole lot of cursing and honking from people who caught up behind them. "We don't want them running you off the road."

Peterson brought flats of potted plants from his trunk and opened the rear door of the hearse to slide them in. "Cynthia was waiting by her gate," he said. "Told us she sat bolt upright in the middle of the night and decided we couldn't go without flowers for Martin's journey home." Since it was not yet fully daylight, the flowers were closed up so tight it was impossible to guess what sort they might turn out to be. Arvo tried out a few names — gladiolus, dahlia, chrysanthemum, peony — but neither Peterson nor Herbie Brewer knew one flower from another. "So long as they aren't those evil-smelling lilies you get at funerals," Arvo said. "Cynthia or no Cynthia, I'd throw the stinking things straight into the ditch."

For the time being, these had no smell at all, and did not resemble anything that any of them had ever seen.

It was obvious now that he would not be making the journey alone. Both Peterson and Herbie were wearing striped shirts and sports jackets. Clearly the three of them were in this rescue mission together. "I'll keep close to the side of the road," he said, once he'd hung Herbie's sign off the rear bumper. "You do the same up ahead. That way, the traffic can see when it's safe to pass."

He put his tool box on the seat beside him — his mother would have called it his *Sampo*, knowing that he had built it himself, like the legendary Ilmarinen, though this had been made from a length of oak rather than a plough blade heated in a forge. His good-luck charm. He climbed in behind the wheel again and started her up. Once he'd driven out of the shed, then closed and locked the door behind him, he said, "Let's go! Martin may not be in any hurry but I've got things to get back to." There was a '49 Meteor out back that hadn't counted on him going off on a trip.

But before they'd started moving, Cynthia drove in and pulled up beside them in the '89 Honda Arvo had found abandoned in a gravel pit and spent one Christmas week bringing back to life. Had she decided to come along too?

She left her motor running while she got out of the car to hand him a tin box. "My banana loaf, as promised!" she said. "Already sliced. Something for when you stop for a break. I forgot to give it to Bert with the flowers." Her face was a little flushed, like a young girl excited by her own generosity. She'd had a reputation as a no-nonsense teacher, but in retirement she'd never been anything but generous and kindly-intended. Before getting back in her car she put a hand

54

on his and squeezed. "You're a good man, Arvo — going to all this trouble for our Martin. Make sure you come back safe."

She winked, as though she suspected he was up to some sort of mischief but couldn't find it in herself to object.

They would take the Old Highway that wandered leisurely along the coastline rather than the inland freeway where they'd be constantly buffeted by blasts of wind from trucks roaring past at speeds the makers of a 1930 vehicle could not have imagined. On the Old Highway there would be less traffic and, except for the odd lunatic, most of it slower. This meant they would be travelling past small farms and threading their way through towns and villages, never far from civilization.

The sky was without clouds but still pale, as it often was this early on summer mornings.

Before leaving Portuguese Creek behind they passed several small stump ranches with their green fields and large gardens, their houses out front too close to the highway, with barns and chicken coops and horse paddocks behind. They passed a series of garden stalls at the side of the road selling baskets of raspberries and boxes of yellow squash and long beans.

When they had begun a straight stretch of highway that passed by the long field of a potato farm, Cynthia drove past in her Honda, honking and waving and going far too fast, then disappeared beyond the Henry J and around the corner. If she was heading in to town, Arvo thought, she would discover the stores were not yet open.

Of course she would know this. She must be on a mission of mercy, answering a call for help from one of her lazy nephews.

He followed the Henry J down the highway at a steady pace, but soon grew tired of giving a return salute to all those who yahooed and waved an arm out the window while passing him. He made an effort to stare straight ahead and behave as though he were just another of those farmers who drove their tractors down the Old Highway pretending not to hear the honking behind them and caring little that they were causing impatient drivers to go crazy. It wasn't as though he were hogging the road. If they were patient enough to wait a few minutes they'd soon find a break in the traffic and sail by.

At a certain speed, curses sounded the same as praise when flung from an open window.

Some of them would think he was crazy if they'd known what he was up to. Off on a fool's mission? Well, at least he knew that Myrtle Birdsong was still alive. He'd torn out the newspaper article about the new theatre and kept it in his top dresser drawer, along with the accompanying photograph. Even in the grainy picture he could see in her face what he recalled seeing in the girl — smiling eyes, sharp cheekbones, a certain tilt to her head. His mother had predicted a classic beauty, declaring "It's in the bones."

He followed the Henry J down the highway past small farms and the occasional cluster of houses and a long flat-roofed school where children chased one another around the building. The motor ran a little rough but it might still be working out a few kinks.

Beyond a long straight stretch of road lined with farm market buildings, a hitchhiker stood on the gravel shoulder waving a hand in a manner that suggested desperation, but Arvo was not about to invite someone to sit beside him and chew his ear off the whole long way to Myrtle Birdsong's door. Even so, there was little else he could do when he was close enough to see that the hitch-hiker was Cynthia. Her Honda was parked on the grassy patch between a broad-leafed maple and a pasture fence. Peterson and Herbie Brewer must have driven right past without noticing her attempt to flag down a ride.

"You change your mind and want your loaf back?"

"My car'll be safe where it is," she said, lowering his toolbox to the floor and climbing in beside him. She passed a hand across the softness of his mother's blanket. "If you're tempted to whisk me off to sunny California, please warn me now. I'll phone my niece to come by and drive the Honda home."

"You know where I'm going."

"I do," Cynthia said, "but you can't blame a girl for dreaming." She waited until they were moving to add, "Fact is, I decided I was a fool to let you men go off to get Martin and have all the fun without me. My niece will look after the place till I'm back. I warned her — I said, Who knows what wondrous things could happen to me before I see you again! She's the one put California in my head."

"If you were hoping for California, you didn't consider this vehicle. Neither of us is likely to live as long as it would take this hearse to get us there. For the return trip someone else would have to drive, with the two of us laid out in boxes in the back."

"Don't worry," she said, dismissing worry with a tilted hand. "Riding as far as town will have to do. My sister can drive me back to my car. I just don't like to be left out altogether. My brothers left me out of *everything*! Henry used to blame them for all my flaws."

Arvo had never thought of Cynthia as someone with flaws. She could have a sharp tongue now and then, but only when discussing the shortcomings of people who put themselves in the public eye. He knew she had no trouble running that little "hobby farm" without Henry, and had probably been the brains, or at least the common-sense, behind the drive-in movie theatre.

Cynthia had been joking about California, but she was not the first woman to suggest a trip together. Long ago, Margot Pearson — Abner's widow — had invited him to drive her to her brother's wedding in Calgary. He could see no reason for refusing — the woods had shut down for fire season, he had no plans of his own, he was curious to see Calgary, and he had always enjoyed Margot's company at community whist drives and local weddings. They had got along well throughout the trip, which included motel stopovers in Vancouver and Kelowna, so it was impossible now to know what might have happened if she hadn't run into an old flame in the lobby of their Calgary hotel — just arrived from Kingston for the wedding.

As they were passing by the bright green grass of the Lazy Meadows golf course, where town shopkeepers and lawyers took out their frustrations on little white balls, Arvo thought of his father's opinion that it was an activity for men who had nothing better to do with their hands. He had remained faithful to his father's bias even though this particular golf course was owned by Pentti Virtanen — son of Matti Virtanen, who'd been known simply as The Big Finn when he was alive, and brother to the hefty Leena Virtanen who had offered to bake Arvo her famous *kula-kukko* to help him relax after his first game on the family links. He'd always enjoyed a good feed of perch-and-pork loaf and even liked the flirtatious Leena Virtanen a little — but he liked neither the dish nor the woman enough to take up playing golf.

He'd been told that Leena's mother Helvi had been a winner of beauty pageants back in her home city of Kajaani. She'd been much older than the young Arvo when she'd arrived in town, and had offered to overlook the difference in their ages, and even her engagement to The Big Finn, if Arvo would forget whoever it was he was saving himself for and expend some of that pent-up frustrated love on her. "You must be just about ready to explode," she'd said, and made it clear she wanted to be around when this happened. She had a certain way of letting just the tip of her tongue show between her red lips. He had been flattered, but too slow to respond. Her marriage to Matti had cooled her interest in Arvo for a while, but at some point she had let him know that her husband would soon drink himself into his grave, leaving the coast clear enough for even a puritan like Arvo to fill the void. But it had been Helvi herself who'd died soon after that. The Big Finn's heavy drinking did not prevent him from taking a second wife within the year.

No one was out on the golf course this morning. Sprinklers that had probably been going all night continued to send water flying in great wide circles. Arvo thought, as he'd thought many times before, that it was a crime this large piece of cleared grass-seeded property was not supporting cattle, at least while the golfers were home and sleeping in their beds. Expensive mowers would no longer be needed. The cows could be rounded up and locked in a pen each morning before the Mercedes and BMWs began to turn in off the road.

Of course he knew this wasn't practical, but he liked to imagine fat Pentti Virtanen out there every morning with wheelbarrow and shovel, earning his keep for a change. He could imagine a city councillor yelling at Pentti after stepping in something Pentti had overlooked.

Once they'd crossed the river bridge and entered town, the unnaturally slow pace allowed Arvo to notice that most of the single-storey stucco shops — whether they were selling menswear, bedroom furniture, fancy cakes, or children's toys — had a *Reynard Realty* sign in one corner of the window, though there was no mention of the property being for sale. Since Ernie Reynard owned a number of these buildings, he must have convinced his tenant merchants that advertising his business was a requisite part of the lease.

Of course Ernie Reynard was not the owner of the real-estate company only, but was also the owner of a lumber company as well as the construction company that used his lumber to build houses on the land his real-estate company sold, as well as the paving company that finished the roads that led to the houses and stores he'd built. There was a Reynard Realty sign even in the window of the restaurant where Peterson and Herbie had decided to stop. "For a decent cup of coffee," Peterson said, "and a little more breakfast before going any farther at this pace of a lazy snail."

Arvo dropped Cynthia off at the restaurant and pulled ahead to *Buster's Service* for a fill-up. Of course he first had to convince the boy running the place that a vehicle built in the '30s could use modern gasoline if its engine had not been destroyed in the era of leaded gas. In order to survive the volley of questions that followed this, he discovered himself to be a little hard of hearing.

By the time he'd joined the others, Peterson had ordered the *Special Steak Breakfast* and Herbie had ordered scrambled eggs, but Cynthia said she was about to call her sister to come and get her. "I'm content," she said. "I've had my ride. And Arvo refuses to take me to California."

But she returned to the table after making her phone call and sat with the others while they waited for their breakfast to arrive and listened to Herbie Brewer complain about their pace. "I never thought we'd be going this slow. If me 'n' Bert waited here 'til you phoned that you're getting close to Martin's hospital I bet we could catch up before you even found a space in the parking lot."

"Arvo needs you boys to lead the way," Cynthia said on Arvo's behalf.

"Yes Mam," Peterson said to the ceiling. "But I don't see a reason for it. He ought to find his way without us, since this same road that goes past here runs the whole damn way to the city and Martin's morgue."

"Still," Cynthia said. "He'll be safer out on that road with an escort car ahead of him." She got to her feet. "Well, my sister will be here in a minute. You boys go have your fun. Riding shotgun in that hearse was ruining my hair."

Eating their breakfast was an opportunity to congratulate themselves for going on this brave and generous mission. They could have taken the easy way and arranged for a professional funeral director to bring Martin home. Herbie Brewer couldn't see why they hadn't driven down in the Henry J and brought Martin home in a coffin tied to the roof.

"Eat your eggs," Peterson said. "What we're doing is giving Martin the sort of final journey a friend and important man deserves."

They were so impressed with their mission on Martin's behalf that it seemed only right that they spend a little time admiring Martin and recalling his many accomplishments as the local Member of Parliament in Ottawa. It was public knowledge that he had never missed a day in his seat while Parliament was in session. The few times he had spoken in the House he had not been heard because of the shouted insults from the party in power. Though everyone knew that Martin had prepared one fine hard-hitting speech on a topic related to children's rights, it was rumoured that the party leader had insisted on reading the speech ahead of time and then decided to let an MP from Toronto speak on the topic instead.

"Poor bugger," Herbie said. "He never had a chance of being re-elected after they stabbed him in the back."

"He never tried," Peterson said. "He hated the Ottawa winter, he didn't know how to ski, he'd never skated in his life, he felt like a prisoner in his own home — which wasn't a home at all but some rented suite in a big old drafty apartment block. No wonder he decided not to run again."

"He didn't decide not to run again," Arvo said, as gently as he knew how. "Someone in Ottawa decided they knew what we needed better than we did ourselves. They figured he wasn't the one we wanted to represent us, whatever we really thought. What else could he do but step aside?"

"Sonsabitches," Peterson said. "No wonder the country's in a mess."

David Henderson came in through the door, taking off his black leather cap. He stood looking around for a moment, running his fingers through his greying hair. Instead of coming over to join Arvo and the others, he sat in the nearest empty booth and waited for Arvo to join him.

"Excuse me," Arvo said. "I've got a little business to talk over with Dave."

Henderson didn't waste time with pleasantries. He lowered his voice to little more than a whisper even before Arvo had slid onto the facing seat. "Where the hell'd you get that hearse out there? Man oh man she's a beauty."

"Thanks for dropping by," Arvo said. "I made a trade for her, fair and square. You bring me a box?"

"I must be crazy but I just now slid a top-grade oak casket into the back of your hearse, along with a whopping big bill for it. I figure Martin Glass deserves the best and you deserve to pay for it. I just hope you know what you're doing. I just hope I know what *I'm* doing. Just don't do anything that gets us into the papers."

"It's all legal. I've got nothing but Martin's good in mind."

"Man oh man, that's a beauty out there! When you're tired of playing with her I'll take her off your hands and park her out front of the business. People will be dying for a chance to ride in 'er." Henderson's laughter tended to end in a snort.

"Very funny. What I want to know is do we have an understanding? You'll fax the hospital with the proper paperwork giving me permission to bring the body home and turn him over to you."

"I know I know. I heard you yesterday. There's still nothing to keep me from going down to pick him up myself."

"Yes, but then you would be losing any hope of borrowing the Cathedral hearse in the future, once I've delivered it to its rightful owner."

"Who is . . . ?"

"You'll find out once we've taken care of Martin."

"Okay, I get it." Henderson sighed and dropped his forehead briefly to the table. "But you don't need to worry that I'll follow you. I spend enough of my life creeping along the road at a snail's pace; it would drive me crazy when I don't have a corpse in the back."

"Go back and fax those forms. It may take us most of the day to get there. All I want is for them to have the paperwork by the time we arrive."

"Man oh man," Henderson said again, pressing both palms to the table top and pushing himself to his feet. "One hint of trouble and I never talked to you, never even heard of you. You'll be on your own, begging some cop to listen to your improbable tale of woe."

"Just fax those forms," Arvo said.

Once he had paid for their breakfasts and led the way outside, he saw that a short stumpy man in a red plaid sports jacket and a boater hat was sitting on the running board of the hearse. He stood up when he saw Arvo approach. "This yours?"

Before responding, Arvo opened the rear door to check that Henderson had actually left a coffin. Solid oak, by the looks of it, with Cynthia's pots of flowers crammed in the space to one side. When Arvo had admitted to being the driver of the hearse, the boldly dressed man introduced himself as the local realtor Ernie Reynard. "You've probably noticed my signs here and there," he said. "I've been looking for something like this. The perfect vehicle to sit outside my Open Houses with a sign on its roof." He slapped a dainty hand on the hearse's hood. "You have no idea how many people slow down for a look but then take off. This'll get them stopped and out of their cars. And once they're out of their cars I'll have 'em. I'll give you a good price for her — right now, right here." He brought a wallet out from inside his jacket, as though ready to hand over cash on the spot.

Arvo laughed and shook his head and climbed in behind the wheel.

"I can see you're a man who drives a hard bargain," the realtor said, stepping up onto the running board and taking hold of the steering wheel with one hand. "I'll even consider trading you a year-old Lexus for it. Crazy I know, but it's my boy's car and he's gone off to university and don't want it any more." He gestured towards the maroon four-door sedan parked across the street, a giant sign on its roof: *REYNARD REALTY, Homes for your Future.* "You better accept the offer before I come to my senses."

Arvo started the engine. "I have a suspicion," he said, "that a hearse may not be the best advertisement for Homes for your *Future.* Your message could be misunderstood."

"Dammit," the man said. He stepped down from the running board and trotted along beside the moving hearse. "All right then, you will let me be your sponsor for this journey — wherever it is you're going. I'll pay for all the gas this machine will burn and I'll be your escort as well. You have no idea how much business this will bring in when people see my company sign on this lovely artefact from the past."

He did not wait to hear Arvo's response to this, but climbed into his son's Lexus and swung around to pass by and pull up in front of the Henry J, which had already begun to move out onto the road. It seemed that Arvo had little choice but to follow, though the sight of Cynthia hurrying towards him while waving her arms made him wonder if he had misunderstood her intentions.

When he'd brought the hearse to a stop, he said, "You changed your mind?"

But she stopped where she was and shook her head. "I just wanted to let you know I *haven't* changed my mind. In case you started to worry. It was jealousy made me want to go with you. I couldn't stand being left out while you boys go off and have an adventure. But of course I was a fool. I'll stay home and bake for the funeral."

"This isn't just because I wouldn't take you to California?"

She cocked her head to one side to think. "Well. California could've made a difference. But as you said, we mightn't live long enough to get there in *this*." She pressed both hands to her ears when she laughed — always had done, as though she didn't want to hear herself.

"Your sister'll drive you back to your car?"

She'd tilted her hands out far enough to hear. "Don't worry. She owes me several lunches and at least half-a-dozen drives."

As he moved slowly through the last few blocks leading out of town, Arvo could see in his mirror that Cynthia had remained standing in front of the restaurant, watching them depart. But as she grew smaller in the mirror he became aware that he had already accumulated a few followers who seemed uninterested in getting past. By the time he had followed the maroon Lexus and the Henry J past the row of strip malls and gas stations and the houses with *Homes for your Future* signs on front lawns and had got out onto the Old Highway beyond the town limits, a long train of cars and trucks had accumulated behind them, all apparently unwilling to pass. Horns honked, but not, it seemed, with impatience. In his rear-view mirror he could see people with heads and naked torsos out their car windows, waving their shirts about as though participating in a football victory parade.

Only when he'd entered a long slow curve in the road could he see in his rear-view mirror that the train of vehicles following him had grown to include several cars and trucks and a large number of panel vans wearing the brightly painted logos and outright advertisements of businesses — including a well-known tourist resort, a recycling depot, a fishing lodge, a ski resort, a home-moving van, a landscape firm, a building contractor, a pest exterminator and a farm dedicated solely to the cultivation of daffodils. The last of the vehicles to appear from behind a stand of alder was an orange school bus, which pulled out and passed all the others and would have passed Arvo as well if the driver hadn't decided to pull in right behind the hearse and, in effect, lead the parade of hangers-on. This bus, he could see now, was filled with students singing robustly out their open windows — to the fields of cattle they passed and the campers in the wooded campsite, to the mail boxes and bus shelters and private homes and to the clear blue sky and all the rest of the world that witnessed this patient parade down this paved and winding road in the general direction of the city.

CHAPTER 6

⚬⚭⚬

A LITTLE MORE THAN thirty minutes south of town the Henry J suddenly turned off the road and onto the gravel parking lot between a small white stucco grocery store and a sprawling heap of wild-rose bushes. This had to mean that something was wrong. Arvo turned in as well, and pulled up to the right of Peterson, nose to a weathered log meant to prevent you from driving down the pebble beach and into the Strait. A few scrawny poplars trembled from the breeze off the water. What was left of the parade that had followed them out of town slowed down and almost stopped, probably uncertain whether to turn in as well. But then, as though they'd somehow decided all together that the slow-pokes they'd been following had finally reached their destination, they took off in a rush, letting the roar of their collective acceleration reverberate down the avenue of broad-leaf maples.

Peterson rolled down his window and suggested that Arvo wait here for a while. "Get yourself a coffee or something — unless you want to go ahead without us. I promised Lucy we'd drop in to say hello."

"You crazy?" Arvo got out of the hearse to say this. Lucy had been Peterson's wife for a while, but for the past few years she'd owned a chicken ranch somewhere in this part of the world. "You meant to do this from the start?"

Peterson looked only a little sheepish. "Lucy could be dangerous if she heard I passed by this close without stopping."

Arvo had seen enough of Lucy to know she could be dangerous even at the best of times. But would she even have known that Peterson had passed by so close without stopping? "You could've mentioned this before we left home. If they decide to do something else with Martin . . ."

Peterson raised both hands to admit his guilt. "Half an hour? Is that too much for a pal to ask?"

Arvo looked at his watch. "In half an hour I'll leave, even if I have to go without you." Then, as the Henry J began to move, he added: "If you're late I'll phone the police — The Case of the Chicken Ranch Murder."

He was almost serious. He'd once overheard Lucy Peterson threatening to feed Peterson's privates to her hens. She'd also promised to strangle Herbie Brewer, whom she'd referred to as "that balk-eyed simpleton camped in my sewing room." Herbie should have got out here for his own safety but was probably too terrified to think straight.

And why had he agreed to wait? He felt the fool, sitting here like this, a prisoner to Peterson's whim, Peterson's poor judgement. He should have gone on without him.

He started the engine but turned it off immediately and sat where he was for long enough to watch a pair of yellow kayaks slide past: two women, both with long pale hair, one working a little harder than the other. He could hear their voices even for a while after they'd slipped out of sight beyond a rocky point.

He must have driven past this spot a hundred times in all the years since he'd last stopped on this gravel lot. This had been immediately after high school. He'd paused here to debate with himself about continuing south to the city's vocational school for a year-long course in auto-mechanics. It was his father's idea. "If you have to end up working for the goddam logging outfit I don't want you up in the woods where you'll get yourself killed. Get some skill with machines and you'll have a chance at a job in the shop. Mechanics don't get killed by widow-makers falling on their heads."

He hadn't reminded his father that Bobby O'Hara had died after being pinned beneath a truck that slipped off the hoist.

Still, he'd convinced himself to give vocational school a try.

Along with the practical courses in mechanics, he'd had no choice but to take an "English" course, presumably so that he could read directions attached to new parts he would be installing in trucks. But they were expected to read books. Forced to. There was no James Lee Burke on the course. Well, Burke would have been only a young fellow himself at the time. There were no crime novels of any sort assigned, unless you included the story of a sailor deserting a sinking ship to save his own neck when he ought to have stayed to help passengers escape. Difficult, meaty stuff. He'd got through it, but what he remembered best was the depth of the young man's guilt. "Why did Jim jump?" the teacher wanted to know. They were all capable of answering that one: *to avoid drowning when the ship went down*. But — was it cowardice or only good sense? Apparently it was the young man's job to go down with the ship. Of course answering the tougher exam questions meant having to read to the end.

Unlike *Lord Jim* and the other books he was required to read, the mechanics courses turned out to be, for him, almost as straightforward and simple as the arithmetic and basic science he'd learned in elementary school. Even so, he might have jumped ship himself and dropped out in the midst of the fall term if he hadn't caught a glimpse of Myrtle Birdsong in the cafeteria, and learned from others that she was taking a secretarial course. Probably so she could work for her father's business. Whenever he'd seen her after that, she'd been with a clutch of other girls, probably all taking the same courses. He'd worked up the courage to approach her once, but had backed out at the last minute. She'd peered at him as though she suspected there was something familiar about him. There was some giggling behind him as he hurried away.

He'd wondered if the secretarial girls had been required to read the same books as he had. He'd imagined that he and Myrtle could have talked about Jim. She might have had less trouble keeping track of the last half of the book, or understanding why the young hero had more or less asked to be executed at the end. But someone had probably decided that boys learning to take cars apart and put them back together would enjoy a story of adventure on the high seas — however dense — more than they'd enjoy the books given to the secretarial girls to read.

Unfortunately, the next time he'd caught sight of her he'd been crossing the parking lot with a group of his classmates, and one of the boys had drawn admiring attention to the breasts in her white angora sweater. She'd heard, and turned to show her scorn.

Surely she would not be inclined to hold his friend's crudity against Arvo even after all this time. When he'd later forced himself to approach her, she was as gracious as he should have known she would be. She'd laughed about the incident, and waved it off, and had even suggested they meet the following week for lunch without their usual circles of friends. But he had learned of his father's illness the following day, and had not been able to do anything but leave her a brief note before heading home. For good, it had later turned out to be.

The problem with being stalled and waiting like this was that it gave you time to think about this sort of thing. And, with time to think, there was a danger he might be tempted to reconsider this whole enterprise. He could easily convince himself that he was an old fool hoping to work some sort of magic that would revive a distant past that had barely existed in the first place. He could go home or go on alone, but hadn't the heart for either. Instead, he got out and walked across the gravel to the store and bought himself an ice-cream cone — something he hadn't done in years. He'd had no idea it was possible to choose from so many flavours, but chose strawberry out of — he supposed — nostalgia. A childhood favourite.

Instead of getting back behind the wheel, he removed his shoes and socks and parked them on the log in front of the hearse. Then he rolled his pant-legs up to just below his knees and walked carefully down through the beach gravel and waded into the salt-chuck. Up to his ankles was far enough. This water was cold.

He wasn't sorry to be missing out on a visit to Lucy's chicken ranch. He'd never been fond of chickens. He'd never been particularly fond of Lucy either. During her short time with Peterson he'd kept his distance. And Peterson had kept his distance from *him*. Whenever Peterson had come out of the Store with his mail or a bag of groceries, if Arvo had called a greeting from across the road, Peterson would wave but put his head down and head fast for home. Lucy had probably told him to stay away from Arvo's workshop, where life would

71

only be wasted on pointless talk when there were plenty of chores to be done at home. Once the marriage had come apart, Peterson had apologized for keeping his distance.

Arvo was interested, now, to notice his own bare feet become large and white and foreign as they sank into the bed of colourful pebbles. He breathed in the clean salt smell of the ocean, though it was accompanied by a slight creosote scent off the little wharf behind the store. Two red canoes, roped to the short dock, rose and fell with every small wave sliding in to shore. He used the paper serviette to wipe melted ice-cream from his chin while he watched a sailboat, tilted dangerously low, go skimming past.

Several sharp honks behind him. When he turned, he was not entirely surprised to see the maroon Lexus cutting a wide semi-circle on the gravel and pulling up beside the hearse, its roof sign like a grotesque dorsal fin. The horn was honked twice more.

If the realtor had allowed himself to be carried away with the pleasure of leading a parade he must have been disappointed to discover the parade had disintegrated and disappeared from behind him so had turned back to find out why this had happened. He hailed Arvo cheerfully from the shore, then removed his shoes and socks and rolled up his pant-legs to wade in and stand beside him.

For some time neither of them spoke. Arvo decided to keep his mouth shut as long as possible. Gentle waves slapped at their four pale shins. Hairs on twenty toes stood up and waved.

From beyond the gleaming white heap of oyster shells to their right, a pale green fish boat appeared and took its time puttering past in a sort of northerly direction. On the far side of the Strait, the long chain of blue coastal mountains had gathered a woolly fringe of white cloud around their peaks. Arvo suspected that once the realtor decided to speak he would begin by saying "I will offer you all of this — the whole world — if you will only fall to your knees and worship me. Or at least agree to sell me that hearse for my Open Houses."

But the realtor did not offer Arvo the world, though it was rumoured that he owned, or at least controlled, more than his share of
it. Instead, he admitted that this was the first time his naked feet had
been in the ocean since he was a young boy. "Once they built a swim-
ming pool I never went near the salt-chuck again."

"You're a swimmer?" Arvo asked. It seemed the polite thing to do.

"Never mind that. Before my goddam feet freeze off I want to
make you an offer and I'm counting on you to agree to it."

But then it seemed he didn't necessarily want to *buy* the hearse
after all, or make a trade. He offered a large sum of money if Arvo
would agree to rent him the Cadillac Cathedral now and then, on the
weekends of his Open Houses. "I'll return it to you when it's not in
use."

Martin would have rolled his eyes at this feeble attempt at negotiating. Arvo said nothing.

"Name a price and see what I got to say about it," the realtor said.
"Go on — give me a figure."

"There *is* no figure," Arvo said. "You can't have it. I don't want
you to have it. I have someone else in mind for it."

The realtor's brow lowered, suspicious. "Who do you have in
mind? Is this a goddam silent auction?" There was a note of panic in
his voice. "Someone has offered you more than the value of my son's
car?"

"The someone else I have in mind is already the rightful owner."

The realtor's sigh was one of exasperation. "Why am I wasting my
breath on you if it belongs to someone else? Tell me the owner's name
and I'll get in touch myself. Maybe he'll have the brains to recognize
a generous offer when he hears one."

"Sorry," Arvo said. "I don't give the names of my friends to strangers."

The realtor's face was now a dangerous red.

"I'm not a stranger, dammit. Everyone knows who I am."

Arvo could not be tempted to give this man his wish. Once they'd brought Martin home, he would turn around and deliver the Cadillac to Myrtle — immediately, in case the family of loggers was unhappy with his reconditioned Fargo. They might even be foolish enough to go to the police out of spite, which could keep him and the hearse tied up in legal proceedings for years. This could be avoided only if the hearse was back in the possession of Charlie Birdsong's daughter. Papers somewhere in some lawyer's office could be unearthed. The imagined joy on that lovely remembered face would be much more "world" to inherit than anything the realtor could offer.

Now the wake created by the passing fish boat was sending in waves that swelled high enough to wet the realtor's rolled-up pantlegs. He cursed Arvo for being even more stubborn than he was himself, and turned to wade ashore. "I don't take failure lightly, Mr. Saarawhatzitt. You'll be hearing from my men." He said "my men" as though he saw himself as a fascist leader referring to his secret police.

Ashore, the realtor lost his balance twice, trying to pull his diamond socks up over one wet foot while standing wobbly on the other. Eventually he gave up and walked off with shoes and socks in his hands, and sat inside his car to pull them on. When he drove off, his tires squealed on the highway pavement. It was possible the man had experienced defeat so seldom he didn't know how to deal with it.

Arvo had no intention of going ashore now that he had the ocean — or at least this beach — to himself. He breathed in the fresh salty smell, bent to scoop up a handful of water and let it leak through his fingers. Clouds had lifted from the peaks of the facing mountains, revealing patches of snow.

Martin had loved the ocean. He'd lived on the edge of it, swam in it daily even in winter, went out in his boat to fish as often as he could.

74

He'd loved the smell of it, the feel of it against his skin, its colour when he looked down into its depths. "I should've been a seal," he'd said. He'd even looked a little like a seal, with his large brown eyes and pointed face.

It was being so far from the ocean in Ottawa that had made him realize it had been a mistake to allow himself to be elected to the House of Commons. "You'd think I didn't remember where the Capital City *was*, for pity sake!" he'd told Arvo. "Every day I lived there, in my dinky apartment or my office, or even in my back-row seat in the House. I dreamt of buying myself a little one-man sailboat and setting off to explore the islands in the Strait. I'd tie up in Poet's Cove for a couple of days, then move on to Salt Spring for a while — then up to Gabriola, Lasqueti, Quadra, even Cortes. I saw myself paddling up Desolation Sound accompanied by a pod of killer whales. I used to say the islands' names to myself like some sort of prayer. More than once I caught people looking at me sort of strange, as though they thought I was losing my mind. Maybe I was."

Martin hadn't spent as much time as the others in Arvo's machine shop. Though Peterson and Herbie Brewer, and sometimes Cynthia, would hang around watching him at work and gossiping until he had to suggest it was time they go home and let him make himself some supper, Martin had made it clear that he enjoyed the company — though he'd usually left as soon as the conversation circled back to start repeating itself, as it always eventually did.

Before going off to Ottawa, Martin had already been a widower for several years and the long-time owner of the weekly newspaper in town. Since he was nearly retirement age by the time he was elected, he'd sold the business within months, making — for some reason that was never discussed — an enemy of his son, who'd immediately set off for a new life of his own on the Prairies.

Now and then, Arvo had been invited to Martin's place on his own. Maybe the others had as well, he didn't know. At Martin's place you didn't feel you needed to fill every minute with talk when you were sitting on a deck with a beer in your hand, listening to the low cello music from his sound system, and looking out across the Strait with all that sky and water and the facing mainland mountains every imaginable shade of blue. Families of ducks glided past, rising and falling with the waves. Human conversation drifted in from passing fish boats. It was much like having a friend take you to a movie where he provided you with something to drink and maybe to eat but didn't expect you to talk until the show was over. At Martin's you often stayed outside until dark, and even then you didn't want to go in except when you began to shiver from the cold. When it was time to head for home, you settled inside for a while to warm up first.

"I didn't buy this shack and start fixing her up to live in until I convinced myself that living on a boat would be a mistake. I would never want to go ashore, which would mean I'd never keep a job. I'd never stay in one place long enough to have friends. There'd be always one more bay I wanted to tie up in." His house on the beach was his compromise: one foot on the land, one foot in the sea. "It isn't a seal I ought to've been, it's some sort of true amphibian, like the otter."

"Well," Arvo now said aloud to himself. "Damned if you haven't gone and stopped me from doing something dumb." They'd been planning to bury Martin in the ground — like just about everyone else they'd ever known who died — but he should have known that Martin wouldn't like that much.

Arvo had never had anything to do with cremations. He didn't like to think about one now. Turning people into cinders. But obviously Martin would have wanted to be set free on the waves, to mingle with the whales, and to travel back and forth like the otters as he'd done in life. There wasn't any other way to accomplish this that

76

Arvo knew about. Because Martin had been a public servant for a brief while, it might be necessary to invite the newspaper and some town officials for a small ceremony, but there was no reason this couldn't be held down on the beach below Martin's house.

He hoped he wasn't going to have to argue with the others about this. Peterson could be stubborn. Herbie Brewer could be slow to catch what you meant. When it came to making a hundred-eighty degree turn, both of them could be as slow as a steam locomotive on the Company turntable.

Cynthia would probably understand.

By the time Arvo had waded ashore, the Henry J was pulling in off the road. When it came to a stop beside the hearse, it appeared that Herbie was not inside. Instead of Herbie, Peterson's former wife was sitting in the passenger seat. "You remember Luce," Peterson said, getting out. "When I told her about the hearse she wanted to come for a look."

Lucy Peterson was a tall woman with a chin that dared the world to refuse her anything she wanted and an eye that could nail you to the spot. She had been a famous hunter once, responsible for shooting enough venison to keep the whole community fed, and was not above turning both her rifle and her terrifying glare on anyone who dared to ask for a better cut of meat than the one she'd decided to give. Once she'd got out of the Henry J she narrowed her eyes to have a good skeptical examination of the hearse. She neither kicked nor cursed it. Without even looking at Arvo — and naturally without asking his permission — she slid in behind the wheel.

"If I remember Lucy right," Arvo said, "she's capable of driving off and leaving both of us behind."

Peterson shrugged and made a "what could I do about it" face. "When I told her about Martin, she decided to come with us," he said apologetically. Or maybe it was defensively. "She liked Martin. Well, she used to like Martin a lot. Well, she had a bit of a *fling* with Martin is the truth of it — which is more or less why she's my ex-wife now."

Of course Arvo had known about the short-lived "fling" with Martin but didn't want to think about it. "And all is now forgiven?"

"I could never resist that chin," Peterson said. "Nobody can."

"I can," Arvo said. "And what have you done with the balk-eyed border who lives in her sewing room? Did Lucy shoot him?"

"Herbie refused to sit in the back so Luce could sit up front and give directions the way she likes. When he saw she wouldn't budge he decided to stay behind. He said he'd look after her eight hundred leghorn hens — but I think we'll just head back and see if he's cooled down a little. Maybe if he and Lucy can't get along he can always ride with you."

"Fine," Arvo said. What else could he say?

Well, he could ask Peterson to get her out of the hearse before she decided to keep it. "I think she's had enough time behind that wheel. Myself, I wouldn't want to have an ex-wife who looked so pleased to be playing undertaker."

Peterson closed his eyes. "I'll try, Arvo. I'll try."

"If we let her get too attached she'll be telling me to ride with you in the Henry J while she drives the hearse, and *then* you'll see how unimpressed I am with that chin."

Stepping out of the hearse, Lucy said, "That back end with all the windows'll make a perfect hatchery for my chicks."

"Uh-oh," Peterson said.

"I'll take her off your hands and put her out by my gate. Once people stop for a look they might as well buy eggs while they're there. A pretty good gimmick, don't you think?"

"Sorry," Arvo said. "This vehicle is not for sale."

"I never said anything about buying," Lucy said. "Sooner or later you men are gonna feel like a lot of fools, playing with this thing like little kids with their toys. You'll be glad to see me put it to proper use."

"Anyway," Peterson said, clearly uncomfortable. "Why are we standing around jawing like this? Let's get this show on the road!"

"Not without Herbie," Arvo said. "We started out on this trip together, the three of us. We can't leave him behind to look after a bunch of stupid chickens."

Lucy shot daggers but clamped her mouth shut before her tongue had a chance to say what she thought. Peterson walked a few steps in one direction with his eyes on the toes of his boots, then turned and walked back. He spoke sidelong to Lucy, as though ready to jump and run if he had to. "It's not fair to Herbie. It's not fair to your chickens neither, to leave him in charge. Herbie'll start feeling sorry for the chickens stuck in a pen and turn them loose. Your hens'll lay their eggs all over your ranch. Under logs, up in the trees. In the middle of blackberry bushes. Your whole damn investment will go squawking off between the jaws of foxes and raccoons."

Arvo agreed. Suppose someone took advantage of Lucy's absence to break in and steal a laying hen or two. Herbie had little experience with responsibility. He claimed to have delivered newspapers as a boy but his adult jobs had been short-lived, including nothing more demanding than picking strawberries in June, plucking turkeys in December, and now-and-then filling pot-holes in the logging company's roads. He must have panicked when Peterson drove off and left him to keep an eye on Lucy's ranch.

"I'll tell you what," Arvo said. "You two go back and rescue the chickens that Herbie has probably set loose by now and I'll go on down to get Martin on my own."

"The hell with that," Lucy said. "You're not leaving me behind.

I've got my reasons for looking Martin Glass in the eye and telling him what I think."

Arvo looked to Peterson. "You didn't tell her?"

Peterson frowned and lifted his shoulders. "She don't always listen."

"If she thinks Martin's walking out of that hospital on his own two feet, why does she think we're going down to get him with a hearse?"

Peterson looked down and kicked at a clump of weeds that had pushed up through the gravel. "Lucy doesn't always hear what she doesn't want to hear — do you, Luce? She can know things without letting them make a difference. I'm pretty sure that what she means is she wants to say good-bye."

Arvo looked hard at Lucy, who was looking hard at him. "You hear that? Whatever you got to say to Martin you should have told him long ago. You might as well say it to those wild roses over by the store. Martin's ears are sealed. I wouldn't recommend you say anything unpleasant. I especially wouldn't want you to say it where I might hear."

"What a couple of old boobies!" Lucy said, clearly disgusted. "Let's go rescue my chooks before your friend decides he's Moses and sets the captives free. I shouldn't've let him anywhere near my chooks."

CHAPTER 7

HE COULD NOT WAIT here for ever. Lucy was capable of talking Peterson into abandoning the journey in order to do chores he'd promised long ago to do — replacing broken glass in a window, patching a hole in the chicken-run fence, repairing a drainpipe fallen away from her house. She could keep him busy for days.

Peterson may have been hoping to lure Lucy back. What some people want the most is what they shouldn't want at all. Peterson had driven up to Lucy's when he didn't need to, had brought her down to show off this hearse when he could have avoided even mentioning it, and then had put himself in the position of having to go back to her chicken ranch in order to collect Herbie. Yet he had sworn any number of times that he'd rather slit his own throat than let that woman back into his life.

Arvo would admit to a grudging admiration for Lucy's willingness to be generous now and then — though always on her own terms. She might leave a hind-quarter of venison on someone's doorstep — especially if that person hadn't asked for it but had only paused for a friendly conversation in the Store. She had never directed any of this generosity towards Peterson's friends, who'd sometimes claimed his attention while excluding her. Arvo's workshop had been to Lucy what a gambling den might be to another man's wife, Arvo himself both bookie and bartender taking advantage of a weakling's addiction.

Generally, Arvo tended to be most impressed with women whose strengths might be the equal of Lucy's but of a less abrasive nature. He admired Kevin Williams' mother Marketta who, even while caring for her dying husband, continued to take on Community Association positions that no one else wanted. Alice MacEwan had camped out on the roadside for three months in an effort to prevent Public Works from appropriating part of her property to straighten out a highway corner so that drivers who drove too fast could drive even faster without ending up in the ditch. And Cynthia Howard, a dedicated teacher who had given the same sort of attention to running the concession stand at her drive-in theatre as she'd given to her students, was comfortable talking cars, piston rods, and logging practices with the men in Arvo's workshop.

Waiting here was bound to make him irritable. Did Peterson think it didn't matter how long it took them to get to the city? This was obviously just an adventure for him, without any real urgency. It wouldn't even occur to him that they could be making themselves so late they might have to stay overnight in the city.

So why not go ahead on his own? He should probably have left on his own in the first place — snuck off in the night to pick up Martin himself. By bringing Peterson and Herbie with him he was asking for all sorts of problems — especially once they reached the city. Peterson would return from Lucy's place with a long shopping list of items he'd promised to buy for her. The sensible thing was to leave now and hope the others forgot about him, forgot about the hearse, and forgot about their plan to bring Martin home.

But having Peterson and Herbie along could keep him from losing courage. Without them — without Peterson at least — he could end up convincing himself he was a fool who hadn't the sense to let go of the past. When it came right down to it, maybe only the companionship of his friends would prevent him from changing his mind at the last minute and bring Martin home without ever pressing the buzzer beside Myrtle Birdsong's front door.

He'd always been a man who fixed things — machines anyway: logging trucks, steam locomotives, pickup trucks, family cars. He had never worried much about the outcome. Sooner or later you discovered what was needed, made a decision, and either fixed or replaced the part that was causing the trouble. People, though, were another matter. The problem was never easy to recognize and usually far too complicated to fix.

Having to make a decision worried him. Whatever decision you made, you were still aware of the possibility you should have made the opposite one — or might think of a third option altogether. Just the thought of having to make a decision made him so tired he usually chose to sleep on it, hoping that somehow the decision would be made in his sleep or the morning take the matter out of his hands.

Other cars pulled in, other people went into the little store and came out with bags of groceries. If he sat here much longer someone would come out to remind him that this small parking lot was meant only for customers. He could say he was fascinated by the turning of the tide, or the progress of a passing fish boat, but eventually someone would use the word "lurking" and then there would be no end of complications.

If the choice was between waiting here for the others to join him and driving to Lucy's chicken ranch, the best way to avoid making any choice at all was to get back on the highway driving south at the usual pace so that they could eventually catch up. If Lucy detained them indefinitely, he would arrive in the city without them.

But before he'd started the engine, a silver VW Golf pulled up and stopped too close beside him. A woman stepped out and slammed her door but did not head off toward the store. The pleased-with-herself look on her face and the open notebook in her hand suggested he ought to have left before now. She was probably an off-duty police-woman asked by the grocer to check out the malingering hearse-driver. He would be subjected now to an interrogation. No owner-ship papers? A portable license plate? He would be required to accompany her to the station for questioning.

"Just leaving," he said, for she had come around behind her car and put a hand on the lip of his half-door.

"This won't take long," she said. "A photographer's on his way, but I have a few questions I want to ask while we're waiting. For the *Telegraph*."

The town's weekly!

"Sorry. I was just about to leave," he said. "You can call your photographer and tell him to stop wherever he is and turn back."

She was a pleasant-looking woman of about forty, or maybe fifty — he couldn't guess the age of younger people any more. She had freckles, and a mop of reddish hair. She might have persuaded him to chat with her if she hadn't mentioned a photographer. He did not want to see himself or this hearse in the papers. Not yet, at least. For the time being it was no one else's business why he was driving to the city in this hearse.

"We might have had this conversation at your workshop yesterday if you'd unlocked the doors to Mr. Foreman and myself."

If she worked for a magazine or newspaper, locked doors were bound to make her curious. If there was something to hide, there must be something to pursue. "There was nothing to talk about yesterday. There's nothing to talk about today, either, unless you send the photographer home."

"Dammit," she said, and rooted around in her large maroon handbag. When she'd brought up a bright red cell phone, she held it to her ear and turned away. Arvo considered taking advantage of her distraction to back up and drive out of here, but of course she would catch up to him before he'd made the first bend. And then he'd have both her and probably the photographer as well to deal with. She lowered her voice to speak but Arvo, straining hard, could hear enough: "No, no, I'm sure he's serious. I mean it. I can see he's one of *those*."

Arvo didn't know what she meant by *those*. A stubborn old man? A stubborn old mechanic who didn't trust photographers? He probably wouldn't care to know what box she'd put him in.

He got out of the hearse and sat on the log facing the water. He was not going to be interviewed sitting behind the wheel. That would only encourage her to get in and sit beside him, and then there would be no way of getting rid of her. Even if he started the engine and drove out onto the road heading south, she would probably stay beside him, unshakeable, willing to nag at him right to the end of the journey. He'd never been interviewed by the press but he had a pretty good idea they did not succeed at their job without being as hard to shake as a boa constrictor around your neck.

"Lucky you," she said, coming up behind him and stepping over the log to sit too close. "His wife has the car and he was waiting for a cab. He said he would cancel the cab. I hope you're going to reward me for this kindness."

"It would not have been worth the price of a taxi. I have nothing worth putting in that notebook."

"Not even to answer *Where did you find this beautiful hearse?*"

He could handle this. "The hills behind town are populated with any number of abandoned cars and trucks. No license, no registration, no owners. Someone has hauled them up there to get rid of them. You could go up and see for yourself. I've been doing this for years."

One question and he was already saying more than he needed to.

"You found this in the mountains and fixed it up in your workshop."

"Fixed it up and now returning it to its first owner, who probably doesn't even know it still exists and definitely doesn't know that it's back on the road again."

The woman spoke even while writing in her notebook. "And what is the name of this owner?"

"I've answered enough questions," Arvo said, getting to his feet.

"You can't just tell me the name of this owner you're returning it to?"

"Can't." Arvo spoke now from beside the hearse. The woman had stood up but was still on the far side of the log. "But if you keep in touch with Matt Foreman he'll tell you when it's about to be used again for its original purpose. You just might get a decent story then."

"Matthew Foreman knows about this?"

"Matthew Foreman doesn't know a thing, but he will."

"Shoot," she said. An old fashioned sort of woman, despite the modern look in her eye. "I was hoping I'd catch you off your guard, but I can see you're nobody's fool."

Arvo dipped a shallow bow to acknowledge the compliment. "Give my regards to Matt. Remind him that some people take their locked doors with them when they travel. Well, he knows me well enough to know that. You'd think he'd've done the decent thing and told you."

He waited until her VW had gone from sight, then backed away from the log and eased the hearse out onto the road. He could see no point in sitting still any longer. No doubt Lucy had found chores for Peterson to do. Maybe he would stay for the rest of the day.

The highway followed the irregular coastline on the left, sometimes open to the water, sometimes with a stand of firs and low bushes of wind-stirred ocean spray between him and the beach. On his right, driveways went uphill from newspaper boxes on posts to houses that looked out over or through the tops of trees to the water.

A good thing the sky was still clear — except for a few faint clouds to the east. He had his umbrella but in this roofless cab it would be little protection against rain. The people who'd designed this thing must have been thinking of California, or summers-only funerals in Saskatoon.

For a short while, it was possible to see the sea to his left where a tugboat pulled a series of log booms south to sawmills — moving even slower than he was. To his right, the purple hills that rose beyond forest appeared to be naked except for a narrow feathery fringe of timber the loggers had left to re-seed the ground. And, rising even above this, a sharp sloped triangle of snow leaned against the sky. A level streak of cloud might have been jet-stream breaking up in the wake of an airliner heading for Japan.

Ahead, a very large man removing the newspaper from its green box-on-a-post could not be anyone other than Big Andy Carmichael.

Of course he'd known but forgotten that Carmichael had moved down to this area after Eleanor died — to live with a married grand-daughter and her husband. He'd even been down to visit once, a few years ago, in their long grey bungalow up a slope, flanked by a pair of big-leaf maples.

Arvo waved when Carmichael looked up, but immediately wished he hadn't. If he hadn't waved, Carmichael could have been so intent on studying the hearse that he might not have noticed the driver. And he certainly wouldn't have guessed that an antique hearse was being driven by someone he knew. Now, having drawn attention to himself, Arvo had little choice but to pull over onto the gravel shoulder and stop.

More time would be lost.

"What the hell you doin' in that rig?" Carmichael trapped the newspaper beneath his arm and took hold of Arvo's hand to give it a shake. "Driving yourself to your own funeral?" He laughed, but quickly sobered. "Well, I guess I'd rather see you in the driver's seat than laid out in the back. Who you got in back?"

"No one yet," Arvo said, stepping out onto the gravel.

Carmichael dropped his jaw and scowled. "You weren't planning to turn in here?" He backed up a step just in case. "If you poke me, you'll see I'm still alive enough to holler!"

"My guess, you'd poke me back."

Carmichael bent forward to laugh. "You got that right." Then he turned and shouted towards the house. "Iris!"

One, two, three figures appeared above the veranda railing. One of them came rattling down the stairs in a hurry, then marched down the dirt driveway towards them, a skirt swishing around her knees.

This was his granddaughter, a short, dainty young woman — especially short and dainty compared to Big Andy. She stood on tip-toes to peck at Arvo's cheek.

Iris had been followed by a long-haired young man with a fiddle dangling from one hand. He viewed the hearse in a suspicious side-long manner.

"Oh my," Iris said, laying a hand against the nearest fender lamp. "This gives me a funny feeling. All the people that rode in the back of this — I wonder how many you and Granddad knew?"

"I never seen this thing before," Carmichael said, but exaggerated a shiver. He was an enormous man still — as tall as Arvo and far too heavy. He breathed noisily, as though with effort. His face was an unhealthy flushed-up colour, as it had always been, but his white hair made this more noticeable.

"Come on up," Iris said. "We've been practising. You can tell us how we're doin'."

"Can't," Arvo said. "I'm already taking too long to get somewhere."

"Come up for a drink," Carmichael said, slapping the newspaper against an open hand. "This young fella eyeing up your vehicle is Buddy Woods. Him and Iris and Johnnie up there have been practising for a concert tonight. Also Saturday night's Old Time Dance. You can tell them if you think they're ready." He did a few quick steps to demonstrate the sort of dance he meant, took Iris's hand, and let her do a complete turn beneath his raised arm and curtsey to his low bow.

A white Toyota Camry honked as it raced by.

"Can't afford the time," Arvo said, though he knew it would not be possible now to drive off without hurting Carmichael's feelings.

"Five minutes!" Carmichael promised. "Ten at most. We're trying out my latest batch of dandelion wine."

"Not for me," Arvo said, following up the slope. "Chances are I'll get stopped by cops at least once while I'm driving that thing, and I don't want liquor on my breath when it happens."

Clearly impressed, Carmichael raised both eyebrows and grinned. "Well, I see a coffin in the back. If you're forced to kill the cop you've got the perfect place to hide the body."

"C'mon," Iris said, leading the way up the slope. "It's been ages since we've seen you." Before going up the steps to the veranda she added, "Now don't you two start in with your logging talk! I don't care if I never hear 'slack the haulback' or 'damn that whistle-punk' again."

"We promise," Carmichael said. "Anyway, Arvo spent his life in the machine shop and didn't hear much of that bush-monkey talk."

"I heard enough of it," Arvo said, taking the small glass that Carmichael held out to him after pouring from a tall slim bottle he taken up from the floor. "You'd be surprised what you hear when you're bent over an engine or looking up at the underside of a stripped transmission."

Iris lifted a banjo off one of three yellow chrome-and-vinyl kitchen chairs and sat. "We've been practising 'Hard Times' — for something slow while the dancers recover from the Virginia reel."

The young bearded man holding a guitar was not introduced, but nodded to Arvo anyway. Iris's husband. Arvo had probably met him at some wedding or funeral in the past.

"They've been practising out here in the open in case Ralph Stanley drives by on a holiday and likes what he hears," Carmichael said. "They're hoping he'll offer a job in Nashville."

The three musicians laughed.

The fiddler said, "He's serious."

"In the meantime," Carmichael said, "they're getting limbered up for tonight."

Now the two men joined Iris on the kitchen chairs and prepared to continue, he assumed, from where they'd left off. Instruments were placed where they were meant to be; Iris counted softly, nodding her head, "One, two . . ." And then she tore like a whirlwind into:

"*Wi . . . ill you miss me?*"

The two men sang: "*Miss me when I'm gone.*"

"*Wi . . . ill you miss me?*"

"*Miss me when I'm gone.*"

Iris grinned happily as she sang. The bearded husband scowled down to watch his own fingers at work. All three stomped out the time on the floor.

"So," Big Andy Carmichael said, after the song was done. "You haven't told us why you've gone into the hearse business."

"You'll remember Martin Glass," Arvo said. "Died in the city hospital. I'm headed down to bring him home."

"Oh dear," Iris said. "The politician?"

"I heard he'd passed on," Carmichael said. "There'll be a funeral?"

"There will," Arvo said. "Once I've got him back where he belongs."

"Well, maybe these young folks could play for it," Carmichael said. "If you'd like," he quickly added. "But they might not be good enough yet to play 'Hard Times.'"

"We wouldn't play 'Hard Times' at a funeral!" Iris exclaimed.

"Not 'Oh, Death' either, I hope," Carmichael said.

"It will have to *be* . . ." Iris said, and struck another chord on her banjo. Immediately the others joined her. "*Shall we gather at the ri-ver, the beautiful the beautiful the ri-i-ver? Shall we gather at the ri-ver that flows by the thro-one of God?*"

There were more verses to this song than Arvo could have imagined. What seemed at first to be an invitation to a picnic gradually began to sound like a race to be the first to drown, and then a cheerful acceptance of being swept out to sea. He had a visual image of crowds rushing eagerly down from every town and pasture in order not to miss out on the big occasion, lemmings rushing towards the thrill of throwing themselves off a cliff and into the racing current.

Still, he applauded when they were done. In fact, he was surprised at how good they were. Not that he knew much about music. He put his glass of dandelion wine on the floor, hoping that Carmichael was satisfied he'd taken one good sip. There was too much at stake to risk more. "I'd better get a move-on," he said. "I've a ways to go and that hearse doesn't exactly break the sound barrier."

Anything that distracted him from a job for any length of time would soon have his stomach in an uproar. Some warning signs had already made themselves known.

"You have to come back for a decent visit," Iris said. "Maybe we'll have a new song to surprise you with — an original, about a man driving a beautiful old hearse. Where is he going, and why? What is the secret he holds in his heart, so powerful it drives him to the city, and so mysterious that he blushes a little when you ask?"

"Yeah, well," Arvo said. He could think of nothing to follow this.

"Maybe you'll come down this way for an Old Time Dance," Iris said, right behind him as he went down her stairs. "The community hall's just down the road a ways from here."

"I was never much of a dancer," Arvo said. He didn't add that it had been forty years since he'd been to a dance. "These two clumsy feet never learned to take orders from this one clumsy brain."

"He's afraid he'll be dragged out on to the floor by some woman who's a serious threat to his bachelorhood," Carmichael said. "Your grandmother had a crush on him once, before I came along, but she told me Arvo hardly noticed her. Had his eye on some other woman.

Now Iris, did you give him one of your programs for tonight?"

"I did not," Iris said, slapping a hand against the side of her face. "What's the matter with me?"

"Go back and get him one."

To Arvo he said, "You're probably going to look up friends, but if you get bored you might be glad of an excuse to escape. A fiddle concert could save you from a hand of bridge or a TV show — who knows?"

His flesh shaking from silent laughter, he accompanied Arvo the rest of the way down the driveway. When they'd reached the hearse, they shook hands again. "You'll let us know about the funeral? I'll have them practise something. Of course *this bunch* wouldn't know Martin Glass from Winston Churchill, but I always admired the man. I probably even voted for him once, though I don't remember for sure."

"Here you are!" Iris shouted, thumping down the driveway. Since Arvo was already behind the wheel by the time she reached the hearse, she inserted the folded paper into his shirt pocket. "In case you're desperate for entertainment and every movie house in town is showing *Spiderman*! I've thrown in some complimentary tickets to tempt you. Share them around!"

Once he was out on the road again, it wasn't long before he was aware that Iris's singing was going to continue in his head for a while. Would Martin want to hear *Shall we gather at the river* at his funeral? He knew already that he wouldn't. He knew, too, that the damn song was going to play itself over and over in his head until he had someone or something to talk to other than a 1930 Cathedral hearse.

CHAPTER 8

❧

"SHALL WE GATHER AT the River" played itself repeatedly in
Arvo's head as though on some sort of loop. He didn't know all the
words but that did not prevent the song from going on without them
—to circle back and start again, all those crowds of eager people racing down to the river, apparently ready to throw themselves into the
rushing current. You had to believe that somewhere in the background there were folks digging in their heels and refusing to go
anywhere near the "beautiful" damn river.

As he approached the old dance hall where Iris and her band
would be playing on Saturday night, the song in his head was abruptly
overridden by the repeated honking of a familiar horn. Peterson's
Henry J blew past with Lucy again in the passenger seat and Herbie

Brewer's distressed face peering out the back window. He might as well have held up a HELP ME sign.

"Trouble," Arvo warned himself.

Peterson slowed down and pulled over onto the gravel in front of a PetroCan station. By the time Arvo had stopped behind the Henry J, Lucy had jumped out and pulled the back of her seat forward for Herbie to climb out holding a black duffel bag to his chest. He stumbled briefly, but caught himself and hurried back towards Arvo.

Once Herbie had got in beside him, Arvo stepped out and placed a hand on the roof of the Henry J. "Does this mean you're turning back? Or have you and Lucy decided on a second honeymoon somewhere?"

Peterson spoke through his open window. "We don't need a second honeymoon. The first one never really ended. Wore me out is all, after a while."

"It wore the rest of us out, too, listening to you complain about it." Arvo bent his knees and sat on his heels. Bending to speak through Peterson's window was a strain on a person's back.

"But now we've had a sort of rest, we might try 'er again."

"At the chicken ranch?"

"I'm all for moving her chickens up to my place but Lucy's still mulling it over. Of course we could have a big one-time slaughter and be done with the lot."

Lucy's arm swung out and thumped hard against Peterson's chest. He yelped, and then took a long slow noisy breath.

"Well, one way or the other," Arvo said, "I guess we're gonna miss you."

"*Miss me when I'm gone,*" Iris sang.

"How d'you figure that?" Peterson said. "I'll be just a mile or so down the road the same as always."

"Maybe so, but will you be allowed out of the bedroom long enough to come up to my shed?"

Peterson grinned, apparently pleased, probably flattered.

"And what about Herbie? She didn't like sharing the house with him the first time. Has she changed her mind? Have you changed your mind, Lucy?"

"Lucy says it's someone else's turn."

"There is no someone else. Herbie's got no other relatives, you know that."

"He's got friends."

"He's got acquaintances is all — from his road-crew days."

"And you," Peterson said.

Arvo paused, and looked down at the toes of his shoes, still shining from last night's polish. "I'm trying to think of someone with more patience. Herbie's never been inside my house."

"Nobody's been inside your house," Peterson said. "Herbie'll make a perfect boarder, grateful for everything."

Arvo stood up and looked across to the gas pumps, trying hard to think. "You sure there isn't someone you overlooked?"

Peterson's only response was to rev the motor to suggest he was getting impatient with this conversation. Arvo reminded him not to forget that sign on his front. "You're still my escort car."

"All the way?"

All the way could be a little long without a break. "Well, we might be ready for a bit of lunch by the time we get to that, you know, mini-golf and museum outfit with its own restaurant. Curly Hagen lives near. We could call up him and Maureen to join us. You think Lucy can put her spending-spree on hold long enough to eat?"

"So long as Herbie travels with you and not with us."

As soon as Arvo pulled out to follow the Henry J through the brief waterside village, Herbie hauled in a deep shuddering breath and began to complain: "Every time that Lucy's around he throws me to the wolves. He don't care what happens to me, I could've been killed."

Arvo imagined Herbie fighting off a wolf pack. "You mean at the chicken ranch?"

"Look at these scratches." Herbie held out both hands, turned them this way and that to show off his scarlet wounds. He pointed, too, to a long scratch on his neck. "How was I to know the rooster would spot the open gate when I went in to bring them water? I chased the sonofabitch all over the yard before I cornered him in the woodshed. I oughta wrung his neck! But I didn't, I threw him back in the pen."

"You said wolves."

"You know what I meant. I might never speak to Bert again!"

"Let's not think about Peterson. Let's just think about Martin. It's Martin who died. It's Martin we're on our way to collect, so we can throw him a decent funeral."

Once the village was behind them, the highway turned inland to pass by an industrial park where mobile homes stood in various degrees of completion. Abandoned, maybe — there was no sign of any work going on. The chain-link fence suggested some sort of quarantine.

"I never voted for Martin," Herbie said. He'd clenched both fists, Arvo noticed, as though ready to defend himself. "Bert told me to vote for him so I voted for that woman with the long hair down to her rear."

"You voted for Coral Cleland?"

"Me and Bert had one of our fights! Fencing the hayfield. He didn't like the way I handled the come-along. I wasn't getting the barbed wire tight enough to suit him so he shouted at me and I threw the

97

damn come-along into the bush and quit." Herbie hauled in a deep, trembling, and probably self-pitying sigh. "That was the morning of election day and I knew he'd be voting for Martin, so when we got to the polling station I decided to cancel him out. It was safer than clobbering him with the come-along, which is what I wanted to do."

"I guess you wouldn't be telling me this if Martin hadn't won the election. How would you feel if he'd lost by a single vote?"

Herbie's response was inaudible — muttered in the direction of the roadside ditch.

· "So — you got any ideas what you'll do if Peterson really does go back to Lucy?"

Another few moments of silence while they passed by a man and woman shouting at one another across the roof of a parked Toyota Corolla.

"Don't worry," Herbie said. "I won't come banging on your door."

Now Arvo felt a hot flush of shame. Herbie had been every bit as much a friend as Peterson, the two of them always welcome in his shop while he worked. It had never occurred to him to invite either of them into his house.

It was a terrible thing, he supposed, but he couldn't imagine having Herbie live with him. A person would be a nervous wreck waiting for him to break something, or spill something on his mother's starched white doilies — or even *move* something from where he'd got used to it being. Eventually Herbie would start to feel he had the right to change things. How could a person ever explain why this was impossible?

Herbie brought up his bag from the floor and settled it on his lap. "I hope you don't mind swinging past my old friend Sandy Macgregor, down the road here a ways. I got something for him. Used to work together on the road crew. He moved down here when he retired."

"We're heading for a restaurant, Herbie. You want us to miss our lunch?"

"Down the side-road up ahead. It swings around and joins the highway again, close to that restaurant place."

His stomach issued its warning twinges again! Not only would this slow them down, it could lead them off the beaten path where the chance of a break-down could be increased and the results disastrous.

"Turn-offs right up here a ways," Herbie said. "Maybe you should slow down."

"What about Bert? We're supposed to be travelling together."

"Don't worry about him. I told him this would happen. He'll be waiting for us up ahead. At the restaurant."

So he and Peterson had agreed on this.

"I don't like it, Herbie. You sure you don't want to make this side-trip on the way back?"

"Here it comes — you better slow down. Now watch, it's right up here."

"And you won't hold us up, talking old times with your friend?"

"It's right here. This here's the road. *We just passed it!*"

"Shoot," Arvo said. He pulled over onto the shoulder and waited for three angry drivers to pass by. He could see in Herbie's face that there was no hope of persuading him to forget this demand. The Henry J was already far ahead, and about to disappear around a bend. He backed into a driveway, turned the hearse around, and drove back to the turn-off.

This narrow road travelled uphill into forest at an incline that was something of a test for this ancient vehicle. Arvo held his breath until they'd got to where the road levelled out, but then they entered a series of sharp turns, first in one direction and then another. You never knew what might be coming at you from beyond the next corner. A dawdling ancient hearse was an impediment to those that followed on such a narrow road with little you could call a shoulder and a ditch so deep he did not want to risk getting close. Herbie leaned out his side to look back and report, with some excitement, that they'd already accumulated a truck and two cars. You'd think he believed this was some sort of accomplishment. He chuckled, and seemed not to care that the drivers — as Arvo could see in a quick glance — were shaking their fists, while shouting out their open windows.

In silence they crossed a canyon on a narrow bridge with a steel-grid deck through which they could see a river roaring below. The vibrations could be felt in Arvo's teeth.

Soon they were driving through thick woods, mostly tall second-growth Douglas fir and a dense underbrush of huckleberry and salal and ocean spray in creamy bloom. To one side, narrow driveways disappeared into the trees, each with a battered mail box on a post. A road-side billboard advertised luxury suites in a lakeside resort — *coming soon* — along with pools, saunas, tennis courts, television, on-site health consultants, five-star restaurants, and spectacular views. It did not advertise promised improvements to the road.

Up the steep slope to their right, a truckload of logs appeared, raising a cloud of dust as it barrelled down a gravel road and, though barely slowing, swung out onto the pavement a hundred metres ahead of the hearse, heading in the same direction. When the dust cloud had caught up and engulfed them, Herbie pushed his face down inside his shirt in order to breathe.

Once the dust had begun to clear, they could see that none of the logs was anywhere near the size that used to come down out of the woods. In the early days some were large enough to need their own individual flatcar or truck-and-trailer. These were barely broad enough for telephone poles.

"They shoulda been left to grow," Herbie said.

"Ah — but the share-holders down in California or over in China can't wait that long. You could be cutting those toothpicks yourself if you were still working in the woods."

Of course Herbie's only job with the logging company had been with the road crew, but that had been reason enough for him to feel proud of the giant logs they'd sent out back in those days.

Now the woods were interrupted, suddenly, by a row of storage lockers sitting on a square of pavement. A chest of drawers had been set out beside the road with a FREE sign hanging from the top handle. A short distance farther on, a small sway-backed house stood up on short posts, its front wall collapsed in a heap of twisted lumber, leaving rooms and flower-papered walls exposed like the set of a stage play. A wood stove stood on dainty legs amidst a heap of bricks.

"You sure this is the road we want?" Arvo said. "We haven't seen much in the way of population."

"Just up here a ways," Herbie said. "Keep goin'."

For several minutes they passed through dense woods before another gap opened up into a clearing, this time for a corrugated metal shed, a gas tank up on legs, and a pair of dump-trucks with broken windshields.

There had been rain here recently. The rough pavement was wet, the roadside trees were dripping. Yet the only dark cloud in the sky was far off toward the mountains.

For the next hundred metres the forest on both sides of the road was so tall and crowded that driving was like passing down the bottom of a ravine. Then, suddenly, they came to another isolated patch cut out of the woods, this one occupied by a drab paint-peeled one-storey motel, probably long deserted. Limbs had fallen to the roof but not been removed. A metal gutter dangled. Weeds had grown tall across what must once have been a parking lot.

"Turn in here," Herbie said.

Arvo did not mask his surprise. "Your friend lives *here?*"

"Manages it when the owner goes off to Hawaii, but he lives here all year round, does repairs."

Apparently the friend did not believe that doing repairs included using a paint brush. "And this is what — his birthday? You got a surprise for him in your bag?"

Herbie did not respond to this. He waited for Arvo to stop the hearse and back up to the driveway entrance. Then, as soon as they'd pulled up in front of the motel office, he got out and headed for the glass doors carrying his bag.

The neon "Open/Closed" sign on the roof was not illuminated. If the motel had once had a name it had been removed. Apparently the friend did not consider looking after the yard to be a part of doing "repairs" any more than painting the outside walls. Weeds grew tall where a garden might once have been, along the front wall of the building. Curtains were pulled closed in one room but hung torn and lopsided in another.

Arvo assumed Herbie would have an explanation once he'd come out. While he waited, he took a little time to think of what he might say to Myrtle Birdsong when she answered her door later today — or, more likely now, tomorrow morning. He did not want to act as though he expected to be recognized immediately, or welcomed with open arms. He would have to think of something that would make a connection between the old fart at her door and the boy he'd once been. It might be best to remind her that they had run into one another just the once as adults in all the years since her father married her off to the Hungarian. She wouldn't remember this as vividly as he did, of course, but she might recall the circumstances. She and her husband had come north with her father for the funeral of her father's friend — a friend of Arvo's father as well.

He'd been no more than thirty at the time. He'd sat two rows behind her at the service, and had chosen to sit against the centre aisle so that he could speak to her as she left. But the Hungarian had taken her hand as they filed out, and Myrtle had walked with her gaze on the carpet just ahead of her narrow high-heeled shoes. Arvo had spoken her name, but he must have said it too softly — or maybe she'd chosen not to acknowledge it. At any rate, he'd had enough time to see that she had become, as a woman, as pretty as he'd once imagined. He'd had to sit down again and pretend to be praying for a moment, in order to catch his breath, while others in his row turned to leave from the other end of the pew.

But he had gone to the reception anyway, and had waited for the opportunity to approach her while she was sitting beside her husband with a paper plate of cakes and cookies in front of her. Seeing him heading her way, she'd said his name as a question. Squinting — uncertain — but apparently ready to be pleased. When he'd nodded, she stood up to greet him. "Arvo Saarikoski."

"It is."

"You never returned a pen I lent you once."

The accusation was such a surprise he laughed. At the same time, he recognized that it was meant to be a friendly comment, and maybe not even true.

She laughed as well, and put a hand on his arm. "It was probably one of those old clear plastic things that leak all over your hand. Bound to be dried up by now. Let me introduce my husband."

Her husband had not been much interested in meeting Arvo. Perhaps he didn't care that — as she explained to him now — Arvo had saved her life by helping her with her science experiments. The two men shook hands. The Hungarian also did not look interested in having a conversation with the man who had, besides helping with science experiments, sung duets with her at school concerts and turned the pages at her piano recitals. Still, when she gestured to an empty chair across the table, Arvo sat — despite the man's unfriendly scowl.

"And so," she said, "did you become the doctor you said you wanted to be? An eye doctor, I think you had in mind."

"I said that?"

She tilted her head and raised her eyebrows. Apparently she thought he was only pretending to forget. And had herself forgotten that they had been at the vocational school at the same time — though, in his case, for only a short while.

"An eye doctor?" he said. "I'm sorry you weren't around to remind me when it could have made a difference." He explained that he'd gone to work in the bush, like most young men in Portuguese Creek. But after a couple of years he'd jumped at an offer to work in the machine shop. A mechanic. "A grease monkey now. I lie on my back under trucks and steam engines, with grease on my hands and oil dripping on my face."

He showed her his right hand, which even after the morning's harsh loofah scrub in the sauna had fine dark lines in the creases of his palms.

"All the better to tell your future," she said, taking the hand in hers. "Let me see."

It was her husband's opinion that forecasting futures during a funeral was in bad taste. "Today, it is enough just to *have* a future — when your old friend has just been shut up in a coffin."

"But *Arvo* is not in a coffin." She dismissed her husband's concern without so much as looking at him. "I can clearly see in this palm that he will soon marry a lady grease monkey and have several baby grease monkeys and live happily ever after."

"As happy as you?" Arvo said.

The husband had turned to talk to the gentleman on his other side.

"Of course," she said, as though the question was of little importance and someone in the far corner more interesting.

How long was he supposed to sit here waiting for Herbie to return from the motel? Had he forgotten this visit was not their final destination? There was lunch with the Hagens, he hoped, and then the rest of the journey to the city. Herbie had been known to lose track of time. A half hour was little different from a full morning to him, who had never had to punch a time clock and had depended on Bert Peterson to get him out of the house in time to catch the Company's crummy for his ride to work.

He stepped out of the hearse and followed the weed-infested strip of broken pavement to the main door. Who would choose to stay in this neglected building, up this awful back road?

Inside the bare office a young woman in a blue smock was vacuuming the faded orange carpet. She turned off her machine and pushed a wrist back over her hair. "I wondered how long you would sit out there," she said, and shook her curls about. "We don't get many visitors arriving in a hearse!" She altered her voice as though speaking only to herself: "Of course there've been one or two who left in one!"

Arvo did not say that he was surprised to hear that visitors arrived here at all, by whatever means. Well, there was a pickup parked in the meagre shade of the apple tree, though this could belong to the manager. Or this housekeeper. Or someone planning to demolish the place.

"My friend seems to have disappeared," he said. "I saw him go through this door but he may have been captured and sent to fight in the Middle East since then."

"If he's fighting anywhere it will be in Room 14," the young woman said.

Of course this little one-storey motel could not have as many as fourteen rooms. The doors down the hallway of its only floor were numbered 11, 12, 13, 14, and 15 as though an entire ten-room wing had been removed, or a second floor planned but abandoned.

He tapped on the door to Room 14.

Something about the old man who opened the door made Arvo think he'd seen him before. The face was broad and raw and flushed up the colour of old brick. The few white hairs on his head stood up and waved around like seaweed anchored to the ocean floor.

Herbie got to his feet from a sagging armchair against the window wall and waved him in. "That's Arvo there. Come on in and help yourself to a beer." To the other man he said, "Arvo drove me here." Then he sat again, cradling a beer can in his lap. "This here is Sandy Macgregor, used to work with me on the road crew."

"Used to be his boss is what he means," Macgregor said. "I don't mind telling you what I just told him — when I seen you and that old hearse pull in I checked my pulse in case nobody told me yet that I'd croaked."

A wine-coloured blanket had been thrown over the armchair, no doubt to cover holes or exposed springs. The double bed took up most of the space, which was made smaller still by the cardboard boxes that lined the walls. A hotplate sat on a little desk beside the bathroom door.

"You didn't say if you'd take a beer with us," the old man said.

"I'm driving," Arvo said. "I haven't the time for it anyway. We've got to get back on the road."

."Me and Sandy been talking about my future," Herbie said. He tilted up the beer and glugged awhile. "He's the boss here till the owner gets back from Hawaii."

"Is being the boss's replacement a tough business?" Arvo asked. "Doing repairs and such?"

"Oh, he don't expect repairs," Macgregor said, grinning as though Arvo's notion had been absurd. "Being boss while he's away just means never leaving the place empty. I don't get to go nowhere till he's back."

He heaved himself to his feet then, and went for the door. "Come with me. I'll show you to your room."

"What's this?" Arvo said.

But neither Herbie nor the old man responded. They led the way out into the hall and down to the last door on the left.

Inside, stale air. A bed and dresser, a chair, a door open to a bathroom. The window looked out on a pile of brush someone's bulldozer had pushed together for a fire that hadn't yet been lit. Foxgloves had grown up through the tangled mess to bloom in free air.

"What is this, Herbie?" Arvo said. "You decided to stay the night rather than go to the city with us?"

Herbie sat on the side of the bed and tested the springs. A coarse dark blanket had been thrown over it. Presumably there were sheets somewhere. "Me and Sandy been talking. He's gonna rent me this room."

The old man nodded to confirm this. "Been on the phone a few times, making plans."

"Does Peterson know about this?"

Herbie closed his eyes. "Bert doesn't know nothing."

Macgregor went to the door. "I'll leave you two while I get some electricity into here."

"You known this fellow a long time, have you?" Arvo said.

"I worked with Sandy once on the road crew, that's all. I told you that."

"And people actually live here?"

"Sandy lives here. So do a couple of other guys, off and on." Herbie was silent again for a few moments, looking out through the dusty window. "Sooner or later that Lucy will kick me out so the smartest thing is to beat her to it, move out and spoil her fun."

Arvo felt himself starting to sweat — his forehead, the back of his neck. "Dammit, Herbie, this is no good. We've got to come up with something better than this. You want to be at Martin's funeral don't you?"

Herbie propped the pillow upright against the headboard and slid up to sit with his back against it. "I don't like funerals. They make me sad."

"Thinking of you living here makes *me* sad," Arvo said. "Come on down to the city with us. Visit a museum. Eat in a restaurant. If we don't come up with a better solution and you still don't want to come home I promise I'll bring you here on the way back."

Herbie bowed his head and closed his eyes, presumably to consider this. When he opened his eyes it was only to give Arvo a narrow sidelong look. "Don't promise me nothing you don't mean. You'll be in too much of a hurry to bother with a museum."

"Then we'll try to make the time for it. The rate we're going now we may end up having to stay overnight. We could look for somewhere close to a museum."

"Well," Herbie said.

"Your friend will hold this room for you till we're on our way back, if you still want it then."

"Don't worry," Herbie said. "I'll still want it. Nothing's gonna change that."

CHAPTER 9

❦

SANDY MACGREGOR walked out through the lobby with them but said goodbye on the front step, shaking Arvo's hand and then Herbie's, while promising to keep Herbie's room for him. Arvo resisted the urge to ask who he'd be keeping it *from*? Who did he think would not only want to stay in a place like this but would insist on having the room with its view of that giant pile of dead trees and tangled roots?

At first he thought that being surprised and upset had caused him to forget where he'd left the hearse. Had he not parked it in the shade of that old apple tree? A chill of panic swept through him.

"What the hell is going on? Where's the hearse?"

Sandy Macgregor hadn't yet gone inside. "What hearse is that?"

"Have you got people that park cars out of sight like some fancy hotel?"

"Nobody's here this week but me — and the cleaning lady." The cleaning lady's vacuum cleaner could be heard roaring somewhere inside. Apparently she hadn't driven off in the hearse — unless, of course, she'd left the vacuum cleaner on in order to fool them while she made her getaway.

Sandy looked a bit blank, as though it was someone else's turn to explain the situation. When no one did, he said, "I suppose it could've been that Enright bunch down the road. They drove off with Buddy Williams' Saturn once."

Arvo felt his stomach knot up. "You've got neighbours with a habit of stealing cars?"

Sandy Macgregor kicked at a clump of grass. "Not exactly neighbours."

"What does 'not exactly' mean to people on this road?"

"They could be far away by now."

"They can't be far away. Not even thieves could make that hearse go any faster than a crawl."

Sandy ran a palm over his stubbly jaw. "Enrights probably can. They could've been driving by in their old tow-truck when they seen your hearse. They're a big old family farther down the road."

"With a reputation for stealing?"

"I heard their old man was dying. Maybe he finally done it. That bunch wouldn't think twice about stealing another man's hearse if it meant saving money on a funeral. You stay put, I'll get my truck."

"This is my fault," Herbie said.

Arvo did not respond. What could he say that he wouldn't later regret?

Crammed into the cab of Sandy Macgregor's pickup — Herbie in the middle — they sped down the rough pavement in silence, all three staring intensely ahead.

"How far could they get?" Arvo said. "I couldn't've been inside for more than ten or fifteen minutes!"

Sandy's body language told you he was only going through the motions to be polite, he knew they would never find the hearse, he probably even knew where the thieves had stashed it by now. He might have been in on the theft himself but wanted to impress his future renter with his willingness to be helpful.

"Watch out," Herbie said. "Looks like pavement ends."

"It does," Sandy Macgregor said. "Hold on."

All three bounced off the seat as the truck jolted down off the pavement onto coarse gravel, though Arvo was the only one whose head hit the roof. Maybe this would knock some sense into his noggin, he thought. How was it that his life could sometimes seem like one detour after another? Maybe this was something that happened to people who lived alone — no partner to give him a poke, reminding him to show a little backbone.

The gravel had been sprayed with oil, which he supposed would keep the dust down but did nothing to stop the stones from throwing themselves at the underside of the truck.

Something in the truck bed bounced and rattled and bashed about. Through the small back window Arvo could see three metal garbage cans crashing against one another, sliding and rolling and bouncing off the sides of the truck-bed.

The sense of unease he'd felt when they'd left the highway had become something much worse. They had not only got themselves off the intended track, they had lost Myrtle Birdsong's hearse. He felt a little crazy to find himself on his absurd chase, trusting Sandy

Macgregor and this rough road to take him to the Cadillac hearse so they could deliver it back to civilization.

Herbie ran a hand along the dashboard, clearing away some of the dust. "My grandma owned a pickup like this once. Drove me down the Oregon coast to meet my cousins on . . . I forget which side. We played in the sand dunes until we dropped. It was like being in Saudi Arabia. There wasn't no camels but we rolled and slid and buried my cousin alive. I forget his name."

"You dig him out?" Sandy said.

"I guess," Herbie said.

"You don't remember?"

Herbie shrugged. "He was a mean little shit. I never seen him after that."

The oil was keeping most of the dust down, but the road here was in such poor shape they had to go slow enough for Sandy to see the pot-holes in time to avoid them. The land on either side had been cleared once — but the large stumps had not been removed and new deciduous trees had sprung up amongst them — mostly alder — though Arvo could see one young pine growing out of the top of a wide, tilted stump.

What if the "Enrights" had set off in some other direction in their tow truck — dragging the hearse? Or ditched the hearse somewhere in the bush? Arvo imagined throwing Herbie out onto the road. He would like to put his hands around Sandy Macgregor's neck.

Of course Macgregor was not responsible for this. Not even Herbie could be held responsible. The only one to blame was the old fool who didn't think to convince Herbie that they should delay the visit to Macgregor's motel until they were on their way home.

Despite this frustrating pace, they were gradually gaining on a long-legged young man who strode with swinging arms along the right-hand side of the road. As they came up beside him — Macgregor slowing to a crawl — the young man turned and raised a hand in what may have been a greeting. He smiled wide enough to show most of his teeth as he took hold of the railing behind Arvo's door and hoisted himself up and over to join the slamming garbage cans in the back.

"Hold on tight, Stewart," Macgregor shouted. "This next little stretch could shake you right off of there."

Stewart slapped a hand on the roof to give the go-ahead.

"We should've asked him if he saw a hearse go by," Arvo said.

"Stewart?" Macgregor shook his head. "He lives back in the bush — probably didn't step out on the road till he heard us coming."

What if the hearse had been stolen not by the Enrights to cut down on funeral expenses but by joy-riders whose idea of fun was to drive it through the roughest terrain they could find until it began to fall apart? The coffin would be slamming about in the back, windows would be broken. Cynthia's flowers overturned. The tires would not hold out long against this kind of abuse. Any minute now they would turn a corner and find it abandoned, sitting low on four flat tires.

They passed by a swampy area, where moss hung from living trees, and tall snags scarred by fire stood up in the mud. Arvo could smell the gassy stench of rotting vegetation. He supposed frogs must have been croaking until they'd heard these rattling garbage cans approach.

He tried to keep the irritation from his voice. "This fellow that's sitting between us told me this road would take us to the highway but he didn't mention it was like driving down a dry riverbed."

Of course losing the hearse like this made him wonder about his reasons for making this journey. Was he being punished now for his ambitions or was he being saved from making a fool of himself? In some civilizations he supposed he would have been condemned to wander these back roads for ever, or at least until he'd recognized and acknowledged and paid for the foolishness of his ambitions. Somewhere in his house there was a copy of *The Kalevala* belonging to his father's mother. In Finnish, of course. He would not be surprised if somewhere in that book it would be possible to find someone sidetracked by his own stupidity or absurd ambition onto a road that led eventually to hell.

He'd never read the whole story — he'd forgotten most of the little Finnish he'd picked up from his folks — but he could remember his visiting grandfather muttering his disgust at Arvo's inability to read the country's national epic in its original language — at least this was how his mother had translated the old man's words. Grandson and grandfather could not speak directly to one another but the grandson could recognize disapproval in the old man's eyes.

It was strange to think that if you lived long enough you could see, in your memory's eye, living images of your grandfather as a man much younger than yourself — not frozen in lifeless photos but actually climbing a rickety ladder to the top, or turning a somersault in a haystack, or steering a car with fifty-year-old hands.

Like his mother, his grandfather might have thought of his tool box as his *Sampo*, offering him protection. But had he remembered that, in *The Kalevala*, once the blacksmith had gone to the cold Northland, that "man-eating, fellow-drowning place" — words that sent a chill through Arvo even now — it had been stolen by "wanton Lemminkainen?" Or was it by a sorceress? He could believe a sorceress might be living down this terrible road.

After creeping up a slight grade where the road stayed close to a narrow creek that trickled downhill alongside them, they came to a small field of sloppy haystacks, a clearing in the forest surrounded by a fence of sun-bleached cedar posts that leaned this way and that, causing the barbed wire to sag in places nearly to the ground. Beyond the field a dirt driveway led up a slope towards a tall unpainted farmhouse beside which a crowd had gathered beneath a large blue plastic tarp propped up on tall stakes. A cover against sun, he supposed, or the possibility of rain.

Not everyone was under the plastic sheet, but those who were appeared to be sitting at a long table, probably eating. A great shout of laughter suddenly went up.

"Enrights," Sandy McGregor said.

When they'd slowed down to approach the driveway, Stewart had leapt down off the truck bed to trot ahead and open the gate.

"There's a casket up there," Herbie said. "Across a pair of sawhorses. See — next to the bar?"

"I don't see a bar," Arvo said.

"Over to the left," Macgregor said. "A plywood table loaded down with bottles. There beside it — a coffin with the lid open. That'll be Grandpa Enright being treated to his final bit of air before they cart him off. One hundred three years old. Over forty grandchildren, all of them smart."

"How do you know they're smart?" Arvo asked.

"Because once they left home most of them never came back, except when one of them died. The old man couldn't stop bragging about them. One's a big-time TV announcer now. Another's a banker. It shows you can never know what's gonna crawl outa the woods when you're looking the other way."

A kind of silence fell over the crowd when Macgregor's pickup pulled onto the rutted drive. A few of the men left the others and hurried over. Women stepped out from under the tarp to watch, standing with their arms crossed. A few of them wore aprons over their dresses.

The first man to reach them saluted Macgregor, then came around to welcome Arvo by shaking his hands.

"We've come for the hearse," Macgregor said. "This here is the man that owns it. One of your lot accidentally drove it home. Where you hiding it?"

"We're the Enright family here," the first man said to Arvo. "I'm Jeremy. This here's my cousin Dick. We're gathered here to pay our respects to our grandpa. All of us are the seeds of his loins! Well, some are married to us, some are friends."

"I'm brought you down some drinks," said a chubby young man in a suit. "This here's cold lemonade for drivers." He handed a tall glass to Macgregor. "This here's a taste of Grandpa's blackberry wine for passengers." He handed a glass of dark red liquid to Arvo, who had got out to stand beside the truck. He offered another to Herbie, who'd stayed inside the cab and shook his head to refuse.

"Take it," the man said. "You can't refuse something on the funeral day of the man that made it!"

Herbie was startled enough to accept the glass and drink more quickly than he ought to. Once he'd caught his breath he said, "That was pretty good."

"Now, naturally you've come to pay your respects. Leastwise, you're not going anywhere without. Come up this way. He's waiting. The old bastard, he's probably watching us right now, trying to figure out where he knows you from. He knew everybody once. Hell, he was related to everybody once. Of course he knew Sandy. But not you," he said to Arvo. "You're not an Enright yourself, I take it."

"I'm not. No."

"That doesn't mean you couldn't be related. Enrights have married into just about every breed of human and wild beast in this part of the world. If you went up under the plastic there and called out your name there's bound to be someone shout back *You sonofabitch, you married my cousin's second daughter by his fourth marriage.* Never fails. Any fool can come in off the road and discover he's fifty-seventh cousin to someone here."

"As I said," Sandy Macgregor reminded them, "we hear that this man's hearse was accidentally delivered here this afternoon. He's come to take it off your hands."

"Not yet, you're not," the man said to Arvo. "You haven't said hello to Grandpa Enright yet." He led Arvo by the sleeve up the dirt driveway to the tarp, where people parted in order to let him through to the casket on its pair of sawhorses. Arvo had no desire to gaze down into a dead man's face but supposed a refusal would cause offence.

"Not there," Jeremy Enright said, putting a hand on Arvo's arm. "There's no one in the coffin yet. This here is Grandpa Enright beside it. Great-grandpa, to be exact. Great-great-grandpa to some."

Great-great-grandpa Enright had been wrapped in heavy Hudson's Bay blankets and propped up in a green plastic lounge chair beside his coffin. A knitted wool hat had been pulled down far enough to cover his ears. Only the bare necessities of eyes and nose and mouth were visible in a face so wrinkled it might have been removed and wrung out like a wet rag and only half-heartedly re-attached. Arvo looked with some confusion into this face until he saw that two milky eyes seemed to register his presence.

"Arvo," Arvo said, though he had no idea if the old man could hear. If there was a hand to shake it must have been buried somewhere inside the blankets. At any rate the name was met with no sign of having been heard or recognized, let alone acknowledged.

"Grandpa predicted tomorrow for his day to die, so we decided to have his funeral party while he was still around to enjoy it. He can't exactly take part but he can watch, whenever he's not dozed off."

"He knows what this is?"

"Oh, he knows. We planned it a day early in case he miscalculated, but I expect he'll be right on time. He always has been. We think of it as a going-away party. You're welcome to join us. There's enough food laid out for twice this crowd. We're expecting more to turn up any minute."

Arvo stepped back from the guest-of-honour and turned to Jeremy Enright. "My hearse?"

For a moment Jeremy Enright looked confused. Then, "Oh, dammit," he said. "Howie was so pleased with what he found we didn't want to spoil his mood when he brought it home. He thought he was doing a big favour for Grandpa. We intended to take it back to Sandy's place right after the burial."

"This man can't wait around for that," Sandy Macgregor said. "He has to deliver it today."

"Oh, shoot!" Jeremy said. "We shouldn't have showed it to Grandpa. You could tell he was pleased to know he'd be spending time in that beauty. We put it away in the tractor shed 'til it's needed. Come." He led the way towards a large sun-bleached cedar-shake barn with a sway-back roof. "You knew one of the tires is low?"

"I did not," Arvo said.

This damn road would be the cause. When you thought of how it shook up Sandy Macgregor's truck you could only imagine how brutal it must have been for the hearse. One of those bloody potholes had done it in.

A burst of laughter from under the tarp. Maybe the lot of them were making jokes about the confused strangers who'd come looking for a hearse they hadn't been smart enough to keep their eye on. Or maybe Grandpa Enright had stood up out of his lounge chair to perform a tap dance for his kin. This seemed to be that sort of family.

The guilty tow-truck was parked up beside a sagging barn, its original colour and company identity covered by a dull reddish paint meant for undercoating. In the lean-to shed beside it, the Cathedral hearse sat with its left rear axle resting on a block of wood. A young man sat on a stool nearby with an inner tube laid across his lap. The tire and an open patching kit lay on the rough concrete beside his foot.

A small boy sat behind the steering wheel, looking pleased with himself.

"Get down out of there!" Jeremy said. "Quick!"

The kid scowled, and was not very quick, but when Jeremy raised a threatening hand he dragged himself out from behind the wheel and leapt to the ground. Yet stayed to see what would happen next.

Macgregor explained: "Boys, this here's that hearse's owner that's just arrived."

"We didn't find no ownership papers in her," the man with the inner tube said, without looking up from his work.

"I carry all the proof of ownership on me," Arvo said. He did not add *in my head*. "Rescued her from a life of forced labour. Now I'm delivering her to the daughter of the original owner, who is long deceased."

"With a low tire?" said the man on the stool. "You didn't know any better'n that?"

"There wasn't a low tire when I parked in front of that motel."

"Well, there was by the time Uncle Ernie hauled it here. Lucky we've got a patching kit is all I can say, or the funeral parade would've been spoiled."

"Ummmm," Jeremy said. "I'm afraid this gentleman might not be able to wait around for the funeral."

"The hell you say!" The man with the patching kit threw the inner tube on the concrete floor. "We promised Grandpa a ride and nobody's gonna spoil it for him!"

"Easy, Ryan," Jeremy said. "We can talk about this."

"Talk with who?" Arvo said. "I don't have the time to stand around and talk. I need to get back out to the highway. This little detour wasn't a part of my plan."

In fact even the detour *before* this detour had not been part of his plan.

"Well," said the young man named Ryan, "as soon as Grandpa Enright saw this hearse it was definitely part of *his* plan, so what are you going to do about it?"

Silence followed this. Ryan glared at Arvo. Arvo did not look away.

"I'm afraid Ryan is right," Jeremy said. "It will be a terrible disappointment to our grandfather."

It seemed to Arvo that since Grandpa Enright would probably be dead for his funeral procession, it shouldn't matter much if the plan was cancelled — so long as he still believed he was going to be riding in this hearse. But when he voiced this aloud, even Jeremy was quick to reject the notion. "We don't lie to Grandpa. Never have. We made a promise and we'll have to stick with it."

Arvo turned to Sandy Macgregor. "How far is the highway from here?"

"Half hour or less," Macgregor said. "Well, maybe three-quarters in *that*."

Arvo hauled in a long deep breath and held it, unwilling to believe what he was about to say. It seemed the only way out of this mess, short of calling the police. And he was not anxious to drag the cops into this. If police got involved, the Enrights would not be the only ones with awkward questions to answer.

"If Grandpa Enright would get so much pleasure out of riding in this hearse while he's dead," Arvo said; "wouldn't he get even more pleasure out of it while he's alive?"

Jeremy Enright narrowed his eyes. "What are you saying?"

"Go ask him. Which would he choose — a short ride in this old hearse today while he can enjoy it, or just imagine riding in it when he's dead and may not get so much pleasure out of it. My guess is, one ride around the four sides of that hayfield down there ought to make him happy."

"If it doesn't kill him," Ryan Enright said.

Arvo showed his open palms as though to say "And if it does . . . ?"

The Enrights glanced at one another.

Jeremy smiled. "I could hold him on my lap, I guess. Sitting up front. There's no weight to him any more."

"Unless he'd rather ride in the coffin," Ryan said. "Lid open, of course. I'll have this tire back together in just a couple minutes. Someone go ask Grandpa what he thinks. Wake him up if you have to."

CHAPTER 10

❧

AS HE DROVE AWAY from the Enright farm, Arvo hoped never to forget the look of surprise and joy on the old man's face when the hearse was driven up close enough for him to recognize what it was and even, maybe, to admire its beauty. The noises he made were barely more than squeaks but his family seemed to understand they were squeaks of pleasure. The man may have been 99 percent gone from this world, but there was still enough of him here to anticipate, with something like pleasure, the chance to ride the circumference of his hayfield in a beautiful vintage hearse. The men of his family had agreed that the old fellow ought to have his ride up front on Jeremy's lap rather than behind windows in the back.

Herbie had refused to watch while Arvo gave the old man his brief tour, but sat on his heels with his back against the wall of the tractor shed. "Leave me alone," he said. "I hate all this stuff about dying."

Several of the women had raised objections. Daughters and daughters-in-law and generations of granddaughters were horrified by what was about to happen. They insisted that subjecting the old man to a ride over the uneven surface of that hayfield would result in a sort of murder. No matter that he would have been happy in his final moments, no matter that he was already well over a hundred years old and so weak that he wasn't likely to last more than another day or so. One especially heavy woman dropped to sit on the ground in front of the hearse with her arms crossed and her eyes daring Arvo to inch the vehicle forward. "You'll have to run over me first."

The others did not immediately put their lives on the line, but eventually one young woman said "What the hell," and stepped over to stand behind her sitting relative with her arms defiantly folded and her eyes narrowed as a sort of silent dare.

Jeremy Enright must have recognized the impossibility of defying this opposition. He suggested that the old man's journey be restricted to the slowest possible speed while travelling only a few times around this hard-packed dirt yard directly in front of the old farmhouse.

The women agreed, but only if Jeremy sat holding Grandpa En-right on the front seat of the hearse so that he could get the general idea without being subjected to much of an actual ride. As soon as Arvo had set the hearse in motion at even less than funereal speed, the women fell in behind, forming a column that followed the hearse slowly across the front yard and around the oak tree, singing "Good Bye Old Timer" — which was, if Arvo remembered correctly, a poem about the death of a logger. Maybe the old fellow had worked in the woods at some point. At least it wasn't "Shall We Gather at the Bloody River."

They sang as they passed by the front steps to the farmhouse, and then around behind the house and past an unpainted, tilted, and probably no-longer-used privy, and eventually shifted their singing to "Hark I Hear the Harps Eternal" as they passed through the open doorway to the empty tractor shed, sending chickens squawking and flapping their wings to get out of their way, then passed out the far end of the shed into sunshine again, the women still singing in unison "Souls have crossed before me, saintly / To that land of perfect rest; / And I hear them singing faintly / In the mansions of the blest."

Though the old man had fallen asleep in Jeremy's arms before his short ride was over, his family members seemed to be altogether pleased with themselves. A number of cameras had recorded the journey. The impromptu choir of women fell apart, laughing, then threw themselves into the arms of their grinning men.

Did being surrounded by so many relatives make this final stage in life any easier? The old guy couldn't have asked for a more enthusiastic group of proud admirers taking care of him. Arvo had been an only child without so much as a cousin or a nephew or any family other than his parents in this part of the continent. His first visit to Helsinki had uncovered only one living relative — a very old bachelor living alone in a two-room apartment. Asked if he'd ever married, the old man had thought for a long time before recalling a girl he'd wanted to marry, but he could not remember whether he'd got around to doing it. Only when Arvo was about to leave did he recall that the girl had moved with her family to Denmark.

"You didn't go after her?"

The old man had looked confused. "I suppose I mustn't have."

A person had to wonder if this sort of reluctance or procrastination or plain old-fashioned shyness was built into the family genes.

Now that Arvo was back on the rough oil-and-gravel road, heading at last for the highway, there was the question of how to tell the others — especially Peterson — that Herbie had flat-out refused to go any farther, and that any attempt to talk some sense into him had failed. Herbie would stay in Sandy Macgregor's run-down motel and Arvo had had no choice but to leave him behind to live in a room so small his belongings would have to be kept in cardboard boxes stacked against the walls.

How long could they allow him to live on a road with little in either direction except bush, isolated patches of industry, a few deserted houses, and a row of storage lockers? At least Portuguese Creek had the General Store where Herbie could buy a newspaper and a carton of milk to take home for his porridge. Portuguese Creek also had Peterson, who'd been someone for Herbie to talk to across the table, someone for Herbie to help with a few outside chores and a little housework. And there was Arvo's workshop nearby, where Herbie was always welcome to drop by for an hour or so of talk.

Of course they mustn't allow Herbie to stay away for good, but if Peterson got back together with Lucy and if Herbie refused to live with them again, it was impossible to imagine who might be persuaded to take him in.

Poor Herbie had been so shy when he'd come to live with Peterson — turned inward, mostly silent, unwilling or unable to meet your eyes as though he was ashamed of being himself. He was already somewhere in early middle-age at the time, but he reminded you of a child that had been beaten so often he believed he deserved the punishment and expected you to start beating him too. According to Peterson, the good-hearted old aunt had tried to train him away from his shame, but had not entirely succeeded. Just having Herbie around could make you feel you ought to be apologizing for something. Of course Peterson, who had never been inclined to apologize for anything, treated Herbie just the same as he treated any other inconvenient irritation and Herbie seemed to believe that this was what he deserved.

He supposed there were some who thought the natural place for Herbie was one of those group homes, with supervision. There were a couple of those in town. It was also possible they thought the natural place for Herbie was Arvo's house across from the Store. One man with a whole house to himself! If he was determined not to take a wife — and they must believe it was far too late for that now — the least he could do was take in a boarder, especially a boarder who was a friend and already a regular visitor to his workshop.

He could already hear them: "Saves old abandoned cars but doesn't lift a finger for an old abandoned friend."

The thought of taking someone into his house called up images of that woman from Thunder Bay who'd stepped down off the bus with her teenaged son and made his life a living hell.

He'd been a fool to let Herbie talk him into leaving the highway. Aside from leading you away from the most direct path to your destination, a detour was also a reminder that there was no end of ways in which life could keep you from even *reaching* your destination.

He supposed that to some people his whole life looked like a series of detours. Avoiding something, he imagined they'd say, though to him it seemed that it was the world and the people in it that kept throwing him off track — starting as far back as having to quit vocational school, maybe sooner.

Just as one detour could lead to another, one worry could lead to another worry. He could reach the city only to discover that Myrtle Birdsong had recently set off with a wealthy widower on a honeymoon cruise through the Caribbean. And of course, even before he reached the city he could be stopped by the police, the hearse confiscated, and himself charged with theft, or at least mischief, and subjected to some time in custody before being set free to find his own way home.

Because there were so many things a person could worry about while off the beaten path, the red STOP sign at the highway came as a welcome surprise. So did the traffic whizzing past. Even the sprawling car dealerships at the four corners of the intersection were a relief. Rows and rows of cars and trucks of every colour glittered in the sun. Banners flapped cheerfully from poles, as though to greet him. Giant signs promised bargains and incredible trade-in deals.

It was hard to believe there were enough drivers living within reach of this highway to justify so much gleaming inventory. He was aware that for every new automobile sold from these lots an older one would be traded in and then later bought by someone else whose even older car would be crushed down and sent away for scrap — or, possibly in a very few cases, hauled up into the mountains and abandoned where the salal and Oregon grape and blackberry vines would eventually try to bury it.

Amongst these shiny new cars, sales people turned away from their customers to watch the Cathedral hearse approach. No doubt they were thinking that automobiles this beautiful were not being made any more, certainly not by the companies *they* represented. They must hope he was about to turn in with the intention of trading this vehicle for a brand new BMW.

Relieved to be leaving the detour behind, Arvo raised a hand to acknowledge their admiration. Several men saluted. A woman in a red jacket presented both upright thumbs.

"Brace yourself, Herbie," Arvo said, though Herbie was not here to heed his advice. "We're about to risk everything by driving into a small town that exists for no other reason than to strip visitors of every dollar they've got before sending them home to Oregon or Alberta. When they see us, they won't see a hearse with an old fart behind the wheel, they'll just see a traveller with money burning holes in his pockets.

The sky above was clear enough, the few white clouds moving quickly, as though in a hurry to get out of his way.

Today the sidewalks were crowded with visitors in loud flowered shirts, wide shorts, and sunburned noses — window-shopping, or comparing purchases with other tourists, or studying maps laid out against the walls of their gigantic travel-homes. Some licked at ice-cream cones. The largest tourists shoved greasy chips into their mouths with a sense of urgency that made Arvo think of shoving dry kindling into a stove where the fire was in danger of dying out. He supposed most of them would have asked for "fries" rather than "chips" since they'd have gravitated towards the shops that were identical to the ones they were used to below the border.

Through the spaces between tall glass hotels and squat motels you could see that the tide was out, the bay a wide flat expanse of grey wet sand and shallow rivulets of left-behind water and gleaming ribbons of purple kelp. Here and there, couples walked out towards the foaming waves. Children crouched to shovel sand into their buckets, probably crabs as well.

The restaurant where he was to meet up with Peterson was a former cookhouse still sitting on the skid logs it had been built upon in one of the early logging camps. Some time ago it had been hauled down here, given a new metal roof, and placed near the entrance to the outdoor logging museum — a few acres of woods with a collection of donkey engines, antiquated tools, and ancient trucks on display.

Peterson's Henry J was parked near the cookhouse door, beside a Dodge pickup and a pale green '89 Honda identical to the one he'd fixed up for Cynthia.

Of course it was Cynthia's license plate number. And it was Cynthia who hailed him from near the restaurant entrance. "I stopped just now when I saw the Henry J and was about to go in but couldn't see the hearse," she said. "Where've you been?"

"Off the beaten path," Arvo said. "Decided to sneak up on this place sort of sidelong, like a wary old hound."

"I'm not surprised," Cynthia said, smiling up at him. "You tend to come at most things that way — as though you think the rest of us might bite. A good thing I recognized Bert's car or I'd have gone flying past and disappeared from the world."

Wild honeysuckle grew thick along the picket fence on either side of the entrance to a pathway into the woods. The smell was sweet in this afternoon sun.

She'd changed her clothes since they'd left her behind. Instead of her usual slacks and hanging-out shirt, she was wearing a skirt, with a pale blue jacket over a white blouse. She'd even put on a little makeup. Either she'd driven home from town to change or she'd borrowed these clothes from her sister. In either case she was more "dressed-up" than he seen her since Henry died.

"You haven't chased me down to nag about California?"

"Not necessarily." She looked away and raised her chin as though she might have resented his question. "It's just that sometimes I can't stand to be left out of things."

"Well then, shall we go in and eat? I think I can smell something good wafting out from the old cookhouse."

As they crossed the crunching pea-gravel towards the restaurant he mentioned that he was surprised her flowers had still not bloomed. "In the back there, with the coffin."

"Of course they wouldn't have," Cynthia said. "Not before they're *there*!"

"Oh." You sometimes couldn't be sure that Cynthia was being playful.

"They have a way of knowing." Apparently she was serious now. "You'll see. They'll come out all of a sudden, expecting applause."

Cynthia was a woman whose mischievous eyes suggested she knew things that others could barely imagine, things that could not be explained in mere language. She could read in your tea leaves that a close relative of yours was about to die, and predict the hour of death, but would refuse to give you a name. She engaged in conversations with the flowers and vegetables in her garden much as others did with their pets, and claimed that she could sometimes learn from them about deficiencies in her soil or the foolishness of planting certain flowers against the northern wall of her house. It wasn't surprising that Cynthia would grow flowers with minds of their own, deciding for themselves when they would bloom.

Cynthia had known immediately that the woman from Thunder Bay would be trouble. Naturally she'd hesitated before mentioning this, but afterwards apologized for not warning him. Though you shouldn't take Cynthia's predictions too seriously, you probably shouldn't be foolish enough to ignore them altogether.

He often wondered if she'd taken this tendency to predict the future into the classroom with her. *Your handwriting hints at a career in espionage. Those bread-crusts you're not eating tell me you'll end up working in a bank. I'd eat them if I were you, since math is not your strength.*

This restaurant had begun life as a floating cook-house on Axel Anderson Lake. It had looked then much as it did now, except that it had rested on floating logs beside a row of floating bunkhouses. The hillside there was too steep to build on — though it was perfect for dragging the logs down to the water's edge. Arvo had eaten his "grub" in this building a few times, years ago, when he'd taken the Company boat up the lake in order to see what could be done about a yarding machine's engine, and had stayed long enough to dismantle and completely rebuild it.

From the doorway, he could see Lucy at a large table in the back corner, examining her nails. Peterson had his elbows on the table while his raised fork emphasized some point he was making for Curly and Maureen Hagen. Curly wore the large straw hat he'd worn since returning last winter from Mexico. You could almost forget he was bald. Even from this distance it was possible to see that Maureen's hair was a sort of auburn today. She liked to change her hair to suit the clothes she'd chosen to wear. One day a blonde, the next a brunette. Arvo didn't want to think what colour she went to bed with at night. It was even possible that both of them slept bald. Two shining globes on their pillows.

"About time," Curly said, standing to shake hands. "We were about to give up on you."

Maureen stayed seated and lowered her sunglasses to look over the top at the late arrivals. "Where have you been? The rest of us have eaten. Me and Curly have to be on our way."

"Haven't you been listening?" Curly said to his wife. "Arvo is driving a hearse. It's a miracle he got here at all."

"You're leaving?" Cynthia said, when Maureen rose from her chair.

"Honey, we're heading the same direction as you," Maureen said, offering Cynthia her chair. "I need my city clothes-store fix. And we've got tickets to a concert tonight. We've eaten and had a good visit with Bert and, uh, Lucy. So now we have to run."

"Hnnnn," Lucy said, without looking up from her nails.

"Fiddle concert," Curly explained.

"Andy Carmichael's bunch are in it," Peterson explained to Arvo. "Curly showed me the program."

"Here you go," Curly said, passing a leaflet across the table. "It's in a church. We're on somebody's mailing list. I may still talk her out of going."

This was identical to the program Carmichael's granddaughter had shoved into his pocket. He passed Curly's to Cynthia and dug out his own. On the front of the folded paper was someone's sketch of a tall stone church with a tower and a wide bank of steps up to the front doors. When Iris's tickets fell out on his lap — there were four — he slipped them back into his shirt pocket. Inside, the program promised a junior fiddle orchestra, three songs: *Big John McNeil, The Merry Blacksmith, Celtic Thunder* — unfamiliar titles. A senior fiddle orchestra, four songs, equally unfamiliar. Wilf Carter followed immediately after the intermission, singing 'The Blue Canadian Rockies.'

"Wilf Carter?" Arvo said.

"An impersonator of course," Maureen said. Her tone of voice said, *We're not fools.* Then she put a hand on Curly's arm. "Darling, we need to go."

Iris Carmichael and her Old Time Band were the last act before the intermission. *I am a Man of Constant Sorrow*, was their first song. *Let Us Gather at the River* followed. That bloody river again. *Killing Floor Blues* and other songs were not familiar. The titles could explain why some were willing to throw themselves into the river.

Once Curly and Maureen had left, Arvo began to study the menu for something he could imagine eating. A plate of fried oysters? He was in the mood for something substantial.

"Herbie stayed outside?" Peterson said.

Cynthia looked up from the menu, confused. "Good heavens! I didn't think. What have you done with Herbie?"

"He refused to come," Arvo said. To Peterson he added, "He figured you two were thinking of getting back together and didn't want him underfoot."

Lucy sighed and crossed her arms.

"He stayed behind at Sandy Macgregor's," Arvo said. "Made arrangements to stay in an old dump of a neglected motel. He probably never intended to come the whole way."

"Dammit," Peterson said to Lucy. "We shouldn't've talked in front of him."

"We decided." Lucy's fierce glare was aimed at Arvo.

"Dammit anyway!" Peterson said. Now Arvo was the one at fault. "I'll have to go back and get him."

Heads turned at other tables. What terrible crime had someone committed? Chairs scraped the floor so people could turn to see better. Cynthia bowed her head and closed her eyes.

"Herbie's a grown-up," Lucy said. "He's doing what he wants."

"Shsh!" — from a nearby table.

"He's doing what *you* want," Peterson said to Lucy. He turned his fiercest frown on Arvo, his face an unhealthy grey. "You were supposed to keep an eye on him."

"No," Arvo said, keeping his voice as level as he could manage. "*You* were supposed to keep an eye on him, but you let someone scare him out of your car. He'd rather be in Macgregor's old motel than be treated like someone you could throw away so easy."

"That's it — blame *me*!" Lucy said.

A waiter hovered behind Cynthia's chair, clearing his throat, obviously unsure how to put a stop to this.

"Shee-oot!" Peterson said, pushing back his chair to get to his feet. "I'll have to go back and get him."

"Sit down," Arvo said. "He won't leave — not if it means being the third person in the house."

Cynthia leaned forward to address Peterson "You'll be able to have it out with Herbie on the way home."

Teacher had spoken. Peterson sat but did not remove his angry glare from Arvo.

Suddenly Curly was back, his hand on Arvo's shoulder. "Don't want to alarm you, but if that old hearse is the one Peterson told us about, you might want to go out and check. A couple of youngsters look a little more interested than I think they should be."

From the cookhouse steps Arvo could see that the Cathedral hearse was still parked where he'd left it, but a youth in a black T-shirt leaned in as though to study the instrument panel. Near the back, a boy with orange hair peered in through the glass with hands to either side of his face. Maybe he hoped for a glimpse of a corpse, or the sound of desperate knocking from inside the coffin.

"I'll leave them to you," Curly said. "We've gotta go. You could just shout to scare them off."

Curly could have done the shouting himself, but didn't. Arvo didn't plan to shout but started across the noisy gravel taking long strides, just another diner heading for his car.

Three stout men stepped out of a silver Corolla, all laughing, all slamming doors, *thunk, thunk, thunk*! A remote lock beeped after they'd started towards the cookhouse entrance.

It didn't look as though these two boys were planning to push the hearse in order to jump-start it. This would have been just about impossible anyway, in this loose gravel. And he could see no tow truck waiting to haul it away.

They could hardly be blamed for their curiosity. At their age, given the chance, he would have had his nose under the hood. He would have gone down on his back to examine the undercarriage. But would have kept an eye peeled for the owner. These two did not seem worried about being caught.

"You boys planning a funeral?"

"Jeeeeez!" Whether he had reason to feel guilty or not, the boy leapt back from the rear windows. "You scared me!"

They were young — fourteen, fifteen. Neither of them would have a driver's license.

"I hope you weren't planning to take her for a joyride," Arvo said. "You could run faster than this old thing at top speed."

He'd made sure he sounded serious but of course he could not help but grin. Unless his smile seemed somehow evil they would know he was teasing. Even so, the freckled red-head who'd been studying the controls had flushed up scarlet. "Just admiring her, sir. You don't get many chances to see one as old as this."

"Well I'm almost disappointed I didn't catch you trying to get 'er started," Arvo said. "I could've opened up that empty coffin back there and accused you of stealing a corpse — just to see the looks on your faces."

"There's nobody in the box?" the boy at the windows said, clearly disappointed.

"It could have been something to tell your friends. Accused of stealing a corpse."

His tool kit was still on the floor where he'd left it. Of course Herbie's duffel bag was with Herbie, back in that run-down motel.

By the time the boys had gone off down the trail through the woods and he'd started back towards the restaurant, several women were spilling out through the front door and down the steps to the gravel, where they embraced and said goodbye to one another. When they'd dispersed, one of them started across the parking lot towards him.

She might have been his own age, he supposed, dressed smartly in a green dress, her hair a tidy silver helmet. "I saw you inside and *thought* you looked a bit familiar but now that we're in the sunlight

I'm sure of it. We were in school together. Weren't we?" She laughed a rather apologetic laugh. "Ages ago, of course! It isn't that you look the same! But there is *something*. Arthur? Artie? I hope I'm not making a fool of myself."

"Arvo," he said. "But I'm afraid . . ." Of course he could not admit that he found nothing familiar about her.

"Of course! Arvo. We were in the same class for a while. In the earliest years. Across the aisle at least once. But you must have moved away. At least you weren't still with us in high school. I was Gabriella Morris." She held out a hand for him to take, or shake, or — it turned out — to feel her brief light touch. "Gabby."

He had no recollection of a Gabby Morris, or of any girl who might have grown up to look like this woman — slight, expensively dressed. But still, there was something. Her eyes, maybe.

He explained that he no longer lived in the city, that his parents had taken him north to the country. "Retired now," he said.

"Like the rest of us." There seemed to be a note of regret in her voice. She crossed the gravel space beside the hearse, fished a gadget from her purse, and caused a beep to happen in the long silver Jaguar parked a few metres away. But before opening the door to get in, she turned back. "Did I only imagine you were chasing those boys away from that hearse a moment ago?"

"You didn't imagine it. You may have witnessed two boys being saved from a life of crime."

She abandoned her car, leaving its door open, and crossed to place a hand on the front fender of the Cathedral hearse. She had long nails painted green and several rings on her fingers. She may have had several marriages since they had been in school together. In any case, she had apparently accumulated some wealth.

"I remember this, or one just like it," she said. "When I was a girl. I don't suppose you remember who . . ."

"Myrtle Birdsong was in my class. Our class."

"So you took over the business. Well no, of course you couldn't have! The building was torn down some time after the old man died — replaced by yet another ugly condo."

"But the family home is still there. The daughter . . ."

"Yes, of course. She has a relative of some sort living with her, I think." She allowed a moment of silence to pass while she stared at him. "You're not taking this to *her*." It was not so much a question as an expression of alarm.

He did not want to risk having her phone the Birdsong household. "As you could see in the restaurant, I'm travelling with friends. A test run for the hearse. It's possible it may need more work before I, say, offer it to a museum — which is where it belongs." A lie that had occurred to him only now, since something like it seemed to be needed.

Gabby Morris decided to forgive him. "I'm relieved to hear it. If a man drove a hearse up to my doorstep, no matter how old or beautiful, it would be a shock."

She slid in behind the Jaguar's steering wheel and pulled the door closed. The engine roared into life. The tires crackled in the gravel as she backed out of the parking spot and swung to the right, then moved forward slowly towards the exit, preparing to join the highway traffic.

He hadn't been aware that Cynthia had come up behind him until she'd put a hand on his arm. "Someone we know?"

"A rich woman admiring the hearse," Arvo said.

As the Jaguar lurched onto the highway pavement its rear tires shot gravel out behind.

"She wasn't trying to steal it?"

"A couple of boys were only admiring it," he said.

"We could have used my car to chase them." She looked as though she regretted that it hadn't happened this way. An adventure.

"Yes," Arvo said. She was grinning, maybe a little too hard. "But that doesn't mean you'd be rewarded with that trip to California."

"Well, I could have been satisfied with a drive to, say, Moose Jaw, where I have a cousin I haven't seen for forty years."

"I've been told that Moose Jaw is a friendly town," Arvo said as they started back towards the entrance, "but it isn't high on my list." He'd worked, once, with a mechanic who'd come from Moose Jaw and referred to all other Saskatchewan towns by similar names he'd invented: *Cougar Crotch, Partridge Piss, Turkey Turds, Saskatchewan*.

"Well," Cynthia said, starting back towards the restaurant steps.

Arvo caught up to walk beside her. "Did Peterson say anything more about going back for Herbie?"

"He did. But somebody kicked him under the table and he decided to wait till we're on our way home."

CHAPTER 11

·⬡⬡○

WHERE THE HIGHWAY was about to plunge downhill and disappear beneath dense forest, Arvo pulled over onto the gravel shoulder and stopped to take in the view. Also to catch his breath. His chest had begun to behave as though he'd run the whole distance from home. Nervous, he supposed, now that he was finally about to go down into Myrtle Birdsong's city.

Only if you'd been this way before could you be sure the road would take you somehow through the forest to suburban blocks of condos, shopping malls and gas stations that attended your journey towards the city centre. In the distance, a few of the city's towers rose high enough above the forest canopy to suggest their destination was still where it was supposed to be. The curve of ocean beyond the city was barely distinguishable from the wide clear sky.

He had returned now and then since the move to Portuguese Creek — to visit an optometrist, to look for rare parts for an abandoned Citroen, to see a movie set in Finland that he knew would not be shown closer to home — but he had never approached the city with this uneasy sense that had taken up residence in his gut.

Well of course he'd known all along that he might eventually see this whole journey as something of a fool's errand. So long as arriving at the city had been only imagined it had seemed a legitimate destination: his childhood home, the original home of the Cathedral hearse, the city where Myrtle Birdsong had grown up and married and become a widow in his absence.

And where, of course, she might not be even slightly interested in her father's hearse. Not everyone was sentimental about a remembered childhood or a father's occupation. She might even resent his assumption that she'd be happy to have the Cadillac returned.

She might have remarried, though the woman with the Jaguar had suggested a relative may be living with her. After the unhappy marriage to her father's assistant she may have become distrustful of all men, a woman determined to resist any reminders of the past. She may have become a recluse who would open the door to him with one hand restraining a snarling dog intent on sinking its fangs into his throat.

A ridiculous picture — at least he hoped it was. But he knew that he did not feel as brave now as he'd felt as the boy who turned the pages of her music and helped her clean up her science experiments.

Of course she could ask what had taken him so long. Why should she be pleased that it had taken him so many years to come down to see her, and, even at that had waited until he had an excuse that depended upon her affectionate memory of her father? He could expect to be no more welcome than a total stranger who'd found the hearse abandoned on the side of the road with a *Please return to* note on the seat.

The women in her book club or her gardening circle would have a good laugh at his expense. *Imagine the nerve! Did he think you'd been wasting away all these years, dreaming of his return? A country hick! Was there cow manure on his boots?*

If he could decide that he was only doing a favour for a remembered classmate he might relax a little. There would be nothing then at stake. And there was nothing to say he couldn't still change his mind at the last minute and decide to go nowhere near Myrtle Birdsong but simply drive to the hospital and pick up Martin Glass. Since the others didn't know of his plan, they would never know that he'd cancelled it.

Cynthia's Honda had pulled off the road and stopped behind him. He supposed she might have guessed there was something about this journey he hadn't shared with her.

"Oh my — this view is beautiful!" she said, slamming her door. Cynthia had a way of behaving as though the world's every surprise was a gift meant especially for her. At a time like this you could imagine how she must have looked as a twelve-year-old girl.

For a moment they watched a pair of tilted white sails moving side-by-side along the bulging coast.

"You must be relieved," she said. "You probably wondered if that old thing could bring you this far without some sort of disaster."

"I've kept my fingers crossed."

"Well," she said, placing a hand on his arm. "It can't be easy, puttering along in something so slow. I have to keep reminding myself not to be impatient. After all, nobody begged me to come."

This was true, of course, but now he found it hard to believe they hadn't invited her to come along. She had often described herself as "just one of the guys." It was clear, now, that she was enjoying this as she might a true adventure.

When the Henry J had returned to see why the hearse and Cynthia's car had both disappeared from the rear-view mirror, Peterson and Lucy got out to stretch limbs and calculate aloud how much longer it would take them to get there.

"The chance of running into police will be greater," Peterson said. "We better keep our eyes peeled." He leapt across the ditch, walked the length of a dead log with his arms out for balance, then jumped down to push his way through huckleberry bushes and disappear into woods.

"Needs to pee," Lucy said. She stood on one foot to remove a small stone from her shoe.

Soon, the Henry J again led the parade, with the SLOW VEHICLE FOLLOWING sign out front and with Lucy sitting in Herbie's passenger seat. Cynthia's Honda brought up the rear with SORRY WE'RE GOING AS FAST AS WE CAN removed from the hearse and attached to her rear bumper.

Arvo was not sorry to have the Cadillac to himself. This was how he'd left home; this was how he would arrive. And being alone gave him an opportunity to try sorting out his confused thoughts after that conversation with the woman who drove the Jaguar. If she were Myrtle Birdsong she would probably phone the police. Should he telephone first, to prepare her? Should he wait for morning?

Should he, maybe, forget the whole idea?

The road led them downhill to wind their way through woods and alongside a rushing river and past a roaring white waterfall and a few clusters of houses sitting in clearings carved out of the forest.

But the descent itself seemed to increase the mix of anxiety and anticipation that had set up residence in his stomach.

He did not want to think about the hospital morgue. He especially didn't want to think about Martin laid out in the morgue. To imagine Martin in a hospital bed had been bad enough, especially when the hospital was this far from home. What was even worse was having to ask yourself, now, why you hadn't come down to visit while Martin was still alive. Well, he'd been in that hospital for only a few days, which hadn't seemed so long at the time. If he'd been there a week you might have driven down to visit. You certainly hadn't thought you'd be driving down to take him home in a box.

Eventually the road broke free from forest to enter the first serious evidence of civilization: a cluster of houses on either side of a Corner Store. A traffic light, and then a large shopping mall. At the first service station on his side of the road, Arvo pulled in by the gas pumps, with Cynthia right behind him. By the time Peterson and Lucy had come back to see why the others were once again no longer behind them, Arvo was making use of the water hose to rid the hearse of the dust accumulated during Herbie's detour.

"This is a good place to get ourselves some ice," Peterson said. "It's going to be a long drive home for a corpse."

"But not tonight," Arvo said. He had glanced at his watch and done some calculating. It was late afternoon already. "We're too late to pick up Martin today and get all the way home before dark. We can thank Herbie for that. We might as well find ourselves a motel and get Martin in the morning."

"Can't say I'm sorry," Peterson said. "This driving slow takes more out of a person than I'd thought."

"Let us hope for a motel with more than one available room," Arvo said. He hoped, in fact, for three or four.

"What you really mean is you want to go to the fiddle concert," Cynthia said. "A chance to see the Carmichaels in action!"

"You've got to be kidding!" Lucy said. "On a Friday night, when most of the stores'll be open?"

Arvo recognized that something in him had relaxed. "I'll phone the hospital first thing tomorrow," he said. "Let them know we'll be by to pick up Martin." He glanced at his watch. "There's probably nobody at the morgue this time of day."

"Nobody alive, anyway," Lucy said.

He would put off stopping by Myrtle's place until morning.

With most of the dust washed from the hearse, he could see that despite the few dents and scratches, the vehicle still looked rather exotic — and was beautiful or unusual enough to have drawn an admiring crowd that applauded as he pulled away from the pumps to drive ahead and park in front of the long white two-storey motel next door. Peterson pulled up beside him and offered to go in and see what was available.

"They've only got two rooms left," he said, after coming out of the office. "You think that's enough? One for the men, one for the women?"

Lucy glared at Peterson, but Peterson said he didn't feel like driving all over town in search of another motel. "We'd probably just get lost."

"Are you sure of this?" Arvo said, as soon as the women had gone inside to sign for the rooms. "Lucy and Cynthia in the same room? Neither one is likely to thank you for it."

Peterson's grin was wide. "If they can't get along, one of them could bunk in with us or curl up in the Henry J, take their pick."

Because their rooms were off the second-floor veranda, Arvo claimed the one closest to the wooden staircase for himself and Peterson. Then he drove the hearse up close to the staircase and brought out a short cable from his tool kit. He wrapped the cable around the front axle, then brought both ends around a four-by-four wooden post and snapped the combination lock closed. It might have been better to have the hearse out of sight from the road, but here at least he would be able to check on it now and then without going outside in his underwear.

Though he had often checked the phone books to see whether a Myrtle Birdsong still lived in this city, he thumbed again through the several pages of Bs. And there was indeed an M. Birdsong still listed at the familiar address.

He had no trouble recalling his boyish terror while climbing the front stairs the first time — a practice session for a school concert — expecting to find dead bodies in every room of the house, laid out on tables or stacked against the walls. Of course she had laughed when she noticed his anxious peering about, and had explained that her father's business was kept to a separate building facing the street behind. Though he'd let her ride in the hearse, she said, she'd never been inside where he works. "Though, if I decide one day to follow in his footsteps . . ."

Of course she had laughed, and immediately denied any real interest in the business, though she'd sworn she'd never leave her father for a career in any other city. In fact, he'd later discovered, she had for a brief while owned her own small florist shop in town before marrying the man her father had taken on as his assistant. A man, it turned out, who believed that a woman should not be the owner of a business — even a business that sold boutonnieres, corsages, and bouquets of cut flowers.

While Arvo phoned out to have pizzas delivered — Hawaiian for himself, pepperoni for the others — Lucy brought up a case of beer and a carton of ginger ale from Peterson's trunk and placed them on the little table in the men's room. While they waited for their dinner to arrive, Lucy conducted an informal and un-asked-for seminar on the art of raising chickens. Maybe she thought some lesson could be found in it. "The first thing you gotta know is that chickens are stupid," she said. "You can't expect to get any sense out of them. And you can't expect them to understand or obey an order."

Peterson said he'd known a few people like that. He might even have married one or two of them. "At least with chickens you can put them in a pen and know they'll stay there. They don't go on expensive shopping sprees."

"They're pretty easy to behead if you catch them with an axe in your hand," Lucy said while glaring at Peterson. "But they still go squawking headless all over the pen with blood flying everywhere."

"I'm not sure we needed to know that," Cynthia said. She opened a box of chocolate brownies and set it on top of the television set. "For after the pizza. Baked last night, iced this morning. In case you got impatient and ate the banana loaf somewhere along the way."

Petersen got to his feet. "Shoot! It's still in the car. I'll get it!"

"Teacher brought us treats," Lucy said, not unkindly. "The second thing you need to know about chickens is that if they're given a chance they'll peck one another to death. Watch what happens if one of them gets a little scratch. They won't leave her alone until they've pecked at that spot of blood long enough to kill her."

"Too many people in one motel room could be much the same," Arvo suggested, convinced she had her reasons for bringing this up.

"For all I know they may think they're helping her out by pecking the blood away," Lucy said, "but the fact is, unless you rescue the injured chook, they won't stop until she's dead."

"Sounds like people in stories I've read," Cynthia said. "Shakespeare, the Bible, Faulkner. If I'd known all this about chickens I might have had less trouble getting the students to read."

"Sounds like politics too," Arvo said. When silence followed this, he added: "Poor ol' Martin."

Once they'd eaten most of the pizzas and Cynthia's baking, and had drunk a cup of coffee made in a plastic contraption that only she knew how to use, Arvo suggested that the rest of them could do whatever they wanted with their evening but he wasn't going to hang around a motel room when he could see Carmichael's family performing in a concert.

He could have knocked on Myrtle Birdsong's door this evening as easily as tomorrow morning but he wasn't ready yet. All along he'd assumed he would be making the call as they were about to leave for home, when there was no chance of looking as though he'd come for a meal or a long evening of conversation. If he stopped by tonight she'd feel she had to invite him in, and he'd never be sure if she was being polite even while resenting his intrusion.

"What sort of concert is it?" Lucy said. "Remind me."

"Old time music," Arvo said. "Fiddles and banjos and singing. I have four tickets if we need them."

Lucy's hand dismissed the tickets, the fiddlers, the singing, and those who indulged in such activities. "What I'm going to do is shop."

"Fine," Arvo said, "but Carmichael would be hurt if he found out we were in town and none of us turned up."

Lucy laughed — a little contemptuously, Arvo thought. "You really think he'll notice if you're not there?" When Arvo didn't respond to this, she added, "So go! Once I'm back from shopping I'll keep an eye out the window so your precious hearse isn't stole — though I can't imagine why anyone would want it."

After Arvo had asked the young man behind the front desk to

look up from his book now and then to check that no one was monkeying with the hearse, they drove off in Cynthia's Honda, first letting Lucy off at the city's largest shopping mall and then heading down the street that would lead them farther in amongst the increasingly taller buildings and glass-fronted stores at the city centre. Here the church was easily found at the intersection of two commercial streets, where a line-up of people several abreast reached from the front doors down the several steps to the sidewalk, around the corner of the building, and halfway down the block.

"You didn't tell us we'd have to fight our way in," Cynthia said.

Fortunately, by the time they'd left Cynthia's car in a basement parking garage the line had at least begun to move.

The church they were about to enter was built of pale smooth blocks of stone, with a tower that soared up past the leafy branches of chestnut trees. Peterson shivered. "I never been inside one of these, except for one long boring funeral long ago. You think we're safe from being hog-tied and forced to kowtow to some priest?"

Cynthia elbowed him hard. "You think people are deaf?"

Arvo noticed in this early evening light that she had put on a little more makeup. She must have hoped from the beginning that this journey would include more than just a drive. Would Peterson agree to stop somewhere for a drink afterwards, before going back to the motel?

Once they'd got inside, the long pews were already crowded except for a space here and there only wide enough for a person on his own. It appeared they would have to split up. But Cynthia spotted what appeared to be space in the balcony — enough for three people to cram themselves into a back row if they got there fast.

"I bet the place don't see this many people here on Sundays," Peterson said.

"*Doesn't see*," Cynthia muttered, as though to herself. Then put a

148

hand over her mouth. "Sorry. A habit." Once they'd found and claimed the vacant portion of bench, she said, "Hard seats like this is one reason I use Sundays to do all the things I didn't have time to do in the week."

"Sundays I try to sleep in," Peterson said, "but Herbie gets up early and can't stand waiting long. It's his sighing and pacing outside my door that wakes me."

Cynthia hummed as she studied the program she'd been handed at the door. "Is Carmichael's granddaughter a Carmichael too?"

"She is," Arvo said. "His oldest son's oldest girl, I think. But she may not have kept her name." It wasn't easy to keep from elbowing the large woman to his left. This space hadn't been as wide as it had looked from below.

"Here they are," Cynthia said. "Just before the intermission. That could be good. If we've had enough we can leave right after and no-body's feelings get hurt."

They hadn't long to wait before a happy gentleman in a black bowler hat came out onto the stage and played a rip-snorting tune on a banjo. One of those old-time dance pieces that seemed familiar though you couldn't think of the title. After bowing to the applause, he welcomed everyone to the concert and introduced the first act. With arms thrown out wide he shouted: "Prepare to meet the future!"

The future turned out to be a long line of youngsters traipsing out through a back wall door to take their places across the front of the stage. Not quite teenagers, most of them, Arvo guessed — all holding a fiddle in one hand, a bow in the other, all wearing white shirts and black bow-ties. A lad who couldn't be more than ten, wearing a black porkpie hat similar to the emcee's, took the seat at the piano. He watched the fiddlers get settled. They watched him. His suspenders formed a large red X against the back of his white shirt.

Once silence had fallen over the room and everyone seemed to be settled in place, the boy at the piano nodded once, and up came the bows atop the raised fiddles. Three more nods and as sudden as a slammed door they all flew at once into a whirlwind of fiddling. The boy pianist hunched over the keys, his black hat nodding in time to the chords, his left foot thumping the floor. He might have been an eighty-year-old man from the hills of Tennessee, swaying and nodding and stomping his foot. Bent over the keyboard, he watched his own hands then turned to watch the fiddlers, back and forth, back and forth. The young fiddlers grinned with the pleasure of this joyful race, kept their eyes straight ahead, frowned briefly through a bar or two — perhaps a difficult part — then went on grinning as though this pleasure had come as something of a surprise. For a while a pale-haired boy at the centre played a melody that rose above the others, becoming a sort of game that briefly made him a soloist. When he came down out of his own line of melody and rejoined the others the audience applauded even while the music continued.

The applause, once they'd come eventually to a sudden stop, was a great thundering roar. Could a crowd this large be made up solely of relatives? Faces on every side grinned with pleasure, and several people muttered excitedly to neighbours. No doubt they thought a standing ovation would be called for if the evening had not just begun. What would they have left to do if things got better than this? If he'd stood up alone to applaud they would think: *That man should get out more.*

And probably they would be right. He went to no more than two or three movies a year. He saw concerts advertised in the paper that were twenty minutes from home, and sometimes they were concerts he would like to attend — but he didn't bother going when the time came. He was sure he'd feel out of place if he went alone, but who did he know who would want to go with him? Most had their families to go with. And neither Peterson nor Cynthia would have attended even this concert if it hadn't been a spontaneous part of an excursion — a break from home, a novelty, a sort of tourist attraction. And complimentary tickets of course. Also, the possibility of seeing Carmichael here — someone they knew from up-home — or Carmichael's family at least, performing in front of a room full of city-dwelling strangers.

Once the young fiddlers had played three lively pieces, a string of adults holding fiddles and bows filed out from wherever they'd been hiding and formed two more standing rows behind the young ones. This tune was much more complicated than the earlier ones, and included a couple of instruments Arvo had never seen before. The boy pianist was now blowing into a tube attached to a small keyboard he held in one hand while playing it with the other. Apparently someone had invented a hand-held piano to be operated by lung-power!

Around the curve of the balcony he noticed a group of women of perhaps his own age sitting together in a row. No men, no children. Hair was white or coloured a pale blonde. Chatting, laughing. Well-dressed city women having a good time.

When the fiddlers had disappeared behind doors again, the emcee walked out onto centre stage and took hold of a standing micro-phone. "Now brace yourselves for a real treat, folks. Tonight's special out-of-town guests have come all the way from . . . well, from several klicks up the highway. If I told you they'd just flown in from Tennessee you'd be inclined to believe me once you'd heard them. These are true Country folk! True musicians in the Grand Ole Opry tradition, but from much closer to home. Please welcome the Iris Carmichael Band!"

He supposed he'd never before seen people he knew performing on stage. Especially people he'd talked to earlier that same day. Iris had dressed herself up in a long dress of some striped material. She must have had her hair tied up somehow this afternoon, since he could not recall noticing it this long. Her bearded husband and the other fellow looked much the same as they had on Carmichael's front veranda.

As the program promised, their first song was "There's a Meetin' Here Tonight." Iris began it alone: *"Some come to dance, some come to play, Some merely come to pass time away . . ."* When she came to a sort of end to this, the two men joined in: *"Cause. There's. A. Meetin' here tonight. There's a meetin' here tonight. I know you by your friendly face. There's a meetin' here tonight."*

Once Iris had sung the next verse alone, several members of the audience clapped hands in time with the repeated chorus.

How were the white- and blonde-haired women responding to this? Apparently they were pleased. This time — his second glance in their direction — it seemed the one at the far end had a familiar look about her. The nose perhaps, or the cheekbones.

Well. Of course it would be too much of a coincidence. He found it hard to imagine Myrtle Birdsong as a fan of country music.

Iris's second song was "Will You Miss Me," sung just as it had been sung on the veranda, though with more gusto — Iris singing the title phrase, splitting the "Will" into two distinct syllables, and the men singing the phrase: *"Miss me when I'm gone!"* The desire to be not-missed had taken on considerable energy and determination. It sounded to Arvo like some sort of challenge, possibly even a dare.

Amongst the women friends, the one with the cheekbones could have been Myrtle Birdsong. Why shouldn't this be her? She'd liked music. She'd taken piano lessons from the woman next door. She might not be exactly a fan but she wouldn't be a snob. No doubt she went out with friends occasionally, to concerts of this nature. She tilted her head towards the woman on her right and said something brief — then both women tilted back their heads and laughed.

Of course he could not hear her laughter, since Iris was now into her third song. "Let us pause in life's pleasures and count its many tears / While we all sup sorrow with the poor."

After the fourth "Hard times, come again no more!" the applause was loud enough and long enough to keep Carmichael grinning for a month, wherever he was hiding. Was he in the room? By the time the clapping had died down completely, Iris Carmichael and her band had bowed and bowed again and left the stage to disappear beyond a side door in the wood-panelled wall.

If that was Myrtle Birdsong, would she recognize him if she looked this way? She had probably not even thought of him since they'd spoken briefly at that funeral years ago. She would think it preposterous if he went over and told her he would be driving up to her door tomorrow morning. Behind the wheel of a hearse.

"Thank you!" said the emcee, himself clapping. Then he announced a brief intermission. "Food and drink can be found in the back room. And when you return, our own home-grown version of 'Wilf Carter and the Rhythm Pals.' After that, the Forty Voices Choir will join all our fiddlers for the treat of a lifetime!"

Arvo was glad to stand up and relieve his cramped legs. These old pews had been built when people had shorter limbs. If their behinds were as bony as his they must have brought their own cushions.

"She aint Emmylou Harris," Peterson said, "but she sure knows how to give it all she's got. I was scared her throat might burst right open, she was working so hard."

Cynthia said, "She was lovely! Lovely! And they were having so much fun! I remember that girl when she was just learning to walk.

Her mother carried her around in her arms for so long I thought the child's legs would never have a chance to get strong. And it turns out she was developing a good strong pair of lungs!"

The row directly in front of them seemed to have been chosen by people as their route for filing out towards the aisle and a corner staircase — for the food or the washroom, he supposed, or a cigarette in the fresh air. Laughing, some of them. Chatting happily. Plenty of them were white-haired, his age or older. Two women coming this way were particularly animated, laughing, the taller one shaking her head. She was the one who looked, he thought, a little like Myrtle, or at least how he'd imagined Myrtle might look, based on memory and that blurred newspaper photo he'd once seen. In fact, he was almost certain this could be her.

When she was about to pass by in front of him he said her name, though softly, so that only someone named Myrtle would hear.

Well, she did look up to him and smiled mildly, but gave her head the smallest shake, and walked on by. Of course it wasn't her.

What a fool he would have felt if she'd stopped and he'd had to explain his mistake while a line of impatient people waited behind her! It was enough to make him wonder once again if he was an idiot to think of driving up to her house tomorrow morning. Why would she be anything but confused or annoyed to see him?

She would claim not to remember him. He would have to make several attempts to remind her of who he was, who he had been, and she would apologize for having no memory of him whatsoever.

Of course he could not drive the hearse up to her door in the morning. He would not contact her at all. Far too much time had gone by and since that wedding reception he had never made any effort to get in touch.

"I don't think I need to come back for their 'treat of a lifetime,'" he said to the others. "This day has already worn me out. My whole body is straining for bed."

Peterson raised his eyebrows to question Cynthia, who shrugged. "Fine by me. Though I did have a bit of a crush on one of the Rhythm Pals once, for a while. The original ones. Mike, Mark, or Jack — I'm not sure which!"

They did not leave until after Arvo had found Carmichael chatting with someone down near the stage and had given him a silent thumbs-up. Carmichael had dipped a bow to show he'd noticed. He knew, now, that they had come, had seen and heard his granddaughter putting on a show. He wasn't likely to notice whether they returned after the intermission.

Once they'd returned to the motel, Cynthia went immediately to the second room where, she promised, she would tell Lucy that Peterson had already dropped off to sleep. Peterson stretched out on the bed farthest from the door. "Lucy will be pissed I didn't suggest we share that other room, but you didn't give me any signals about wanting to share this one with Cynthia. It's hard to believe how crazy I was for that woman once. I liked how she was different but I didn't think much beyond that."

"Well," Arvo said. "I guess there needs to be a few Lucys in the world, but we wouldn't want to have too many of them at the same time. I can easily imagine your Lucy pestering a person's sore spot until she's finished him off, like one of her hens. You spend enough time with chickens you're bound to end up behaving like them."

"Says you," Peterson said to the ceiling. "You never had a woman you were crazy about."

"Don't be too sure of that," Arvo said.

"Not that woman from Thunder Bay! Good lord, man! I thought when you pushed her onto the bus it was because . . ."

"Because I wanted her gone."

"Some other mystery woman then." Peterson sat up in bed to have a good look at the man who'd admitted to something he'd never even hinted at before. "Where've you kept her all these years?"

"Up here," Arvo said, tapping his forehead.

Of course he knew he could not back out of his plan for the morning. It had probably been something like this anxiety in his gut that had prevented Martin from visiting his son in Saskatchewan, losing the opportunity to confront whatever problem there had been between them. He had thought: "Not now, but maybe next summer" year after year. And of course now there was no "next summer" for Martin, and a visit was no longer possible.

Arvo was half undressed when the door rattled from someone's knocking. "Yes?" he said, without opening it. "Some of us are nearly naked in here."

"I'm the manager," the voice said. "I'd like a word."

"I'm listening."

"Well. Okay. I realize this is unconventional, but I have someone downstairs who says he wants to make you an offer for that hearse you got tied up downstairs. An *improved* offer, he called it. A fellow in a loud plaid jacket, drives a Lexus? He says his lawyers claim he may have a case for challenging your ownership. I refused to give him your room number."

"Thank you," Arvo said. "Tell him if his lawyers keep on digging they may get a big surprise."

"Yes sir," said the voice of the manager. "But I doubt he will give up that easy."

"Good night then," Arvo said.

"But since I have your attention," the manager's voice said, "I would be happy to make you an offer myself. I can imagine mounting that vehicle up on the roof, something to catch attention and bring people in off the road for the night. This motel's so ordinary it's hardly noticed by traffic racing by. I could rename the motel. *The Vintage*, maybe. "

Had the manager thought this through? Curiosity might cause people to pull in for a closer look but it wasn't likely to make them want to sleep in a bed with a hearse sitting above their heads.

"No thank you," Arvo said. "But you can tell the other fellow I may call the police if he doesn't leave us alone."

Of course he had no intention of calling the cops. A policeman would be required to ask any number of awkward questions, and no doubt expect to see ownership papers that did not exist.

Naturally, now he would not be able to sleep. If the realtor had followed him all this distance, he was capable of hiring a tow truck to haul the hearse away, even if he had to take the staircase with it. The motel manager, too, could be planning to hide it somewhere — pretend in the morning that it had been stolen. This close to looking up Myrtle Birdsong, this close to taking Martin home, he could not afford to take the chance of losing the Cadillac Cathedral now — even if it meant staying awake all night.

And yet — though he hated to admit this — if he did fall asleep there would be some relief in waking up to find this whole business had been taken out of his hands. If the realtor managed to steal the hearse, he might be spared a painful disappointment. He would have tried. Life would continue. He could still remember the golden-haired girl he'd adored from the start. And he would have someone else to blame whenever he was tempted to kick himself for not going through with his plan.

Well, dammit, this was what he had allowed to happen at the vocational school. His pals had joined the group of girls that included

Myrtle Birdsong as they were about to leave the cafeteria, but he had stayed back and watched from a distance as they walked away in a cluster, all chatting. What had he expected? That she would turn and call him over?

She hadn't noticed him, or if she had she'd thought it was his job to haul his lanky frame over to join her and her friends. Instead, he'd gone back to his dormitory room to finish reading *Lord Jim* or something, hating himself for the cowardice. Hating his friends for not forcing him to join them. Hating her for not calling him over.

He wasn't eighteen any more. He was a man with most of his life behind him. How many chances could a man afford to ignore?

"Too bad Herbie's not here to use my bed," he said, now, to Peterson. He laid his dress pants and shirt neatly over the back of a chair, then, in his underwear, gathered up a couple of blankets and dragged a second chair over to the window. "Even if I nod off and slobber with my face against the glass I want them to think there's someone up here keeping watch."

CHAPTER 12

HE MAY HAVE DOZED off briefly now and then, but he was awake when his watch hands made a perfect right angle. Three o'clock. The Cathedral hearse was still anchored at the foot of the stairs. He ought to be able to relax, but recalling his plan for the morning stirred up such turmoil that he did not fall asleep again until some time after four, and only after deciding to pick Martin up after breakfast and immediately head for home. He'd been a fool to imagine anything else.

When he wakened again, this time to full daylight, it took a moment to recognize where he was, and to recall why he was sitting in a chair with his chin on the windowsill and his slimy face against the glass, looking out upon a dull morning parking lot: a few cars, several empty parking spaces. The hearse was still where he'd left it.

There might almost have been some relief if it had disappeared.

When he'd wrapped a blanket around his shoulders and gone down to make sure that all was well, he could see that nothing had been tampered with. No one had removed the casket. Cynthia's flowers hadn't bloomed, but neither had they wilted.

Peterson appeared above at the veranda railing, buttoning his shirt. "They probably arrest people who drive in their underwear," he said. "Or were you planning to wear that blanket to a pow-wow somewhere?"

It was too late to back out. To give up now would make him ashamed for the rest of his life. "Go have some breakfast," he said, tilting his head in the direction of the dining room. "I've a small errand to do first."

Peterson laughed, and leaned over the railing to drop spit to the pavement.

"No sign of the women?" Arvo said, once he'd reached the top of the stairs.

"Probably killed each other by now," Peterson said. "You go do what you have to do. I'll see what sort of grub this outfit's got on offer."

The women had still not appeared by the time Arvo had showered and shaved and dressed, and then gone down to drive the Cathedral hearse off the lot. He followed the street that would lead him down towards the area of town where Myrtle Birdsong lived and where he'd once lived himself: winding streets, older homes on large lots, with a good deal of overgrown and overlapping greenery.

He had driven this route many times in his head, but much had changed in recent years. Whole blocks of houses had disappeared, replaced by shopping malls with expansive parking lots. A once-familiar record store had been replaced by a tall building with a name over the door: *Canterbury Apartments*.

There was too much traffic for so early in the day. But of course this had been his impression every time he'd come anywhere near the city. A tourist bus bullied its way from one lane to the other. It seemed that traffic lights had been installed at nearly every intersection, where pedestrians thrust themselves off one sidewalk in order to race for another.

He turned left at the White Spot restaurant and followed a winding road past the edge of a wooded park that looked more or less as he remembered, then turned left again just past the park entrance and followed for one, two, three blocks. The comfortable old wood-shingled houses, set back behind tidy lawns, were now overshadowed here and there by modern glass-walled houses so wide and tall they looked as though they had elbowed the others aside.

He turned right and followed this familiar road uphill for five, six, seven blocks and turned left. He should have warned her. He should have come here without the hearse, he should have borrowed the Henry J. For all he knew, the sudden appearance of the Cadillac Cathedral could remind her of her father and cause her grief. He would be making himself an intruder in her life, an inconvenient interruption, no doubt causing a confusing mix of emotions.

Why was he thinking of this now? It was something that had happened too often in his life — getting caught up in some project before properly thinking it through. But he could not turn back. To turn back now would mean spending the rest of his life cursing himself for his cowardice.

But now there was this row of Victorian houses for two or three blocks, most of the buildings fairly well cared for. Little here had changed. Front lawns were brief shelves between veranda pillars and a short drop to the sidewalk — probably because the street had been widened, cutting off half their lawns. Rhododendrons bloomed beneath the windows, which were mostly opaque from sheer curtains, with dark drapes pulled back to either side. Settled, heavy buildings. Secretive maybe. He knew these houses. There was probably a crystal chandelier in each dining room, a narrow staircase to the bedrooms, whose slanted ceilings were the underside of the roof. He imagined a little desk or vanity table beneath a dormer window. Some upstairs rooms would be closed off or used for storage.

After parking in front of the familiar Birdsong house with its many gables and stained-glass window panels, he sat long enough to observe how weathered the siding had become — in need of a new coat of paint. The steps to the front door were a bit aslant, or at least appeared to be from this angle. The house had not seemed this neglected the last time he'd driven past, though of course that had been several years ago. The monkey puzzle tree was a familiar relic of another era — one of several brought from Chile when the British moved their naval base north to Vancouver Island. At least this was what he'd been told.

To meet now, after all this time, could be confusing to them both. She would want to know why it took the discovery of her father's old hearse to bring him down to see her. "Had you no idea how this would affect me?" she might say. "You think I need my father's hearse and your ancient face to remind me that I am an old woman now!"

She would not say "your ancient face."

Before he'd made a move — either to go in or turn back — he was aware in his side mirror that the Henry J was pulling up to stop a block behind him, then moving slowly forward as though hoping not to be noticed.

Peterson. And Cynthia beside him. Too damn nosy even to eat breakfast.

Peterson got out and closed his door and came up beside the hearse to ask if there was something about this place that made it worth staring at. "You forget that Martin's waiting?"

"I thought you were going for breakfast."

"You were barely off the parking lot when Cynthia banged on the door, dressed and ready for action. We couldn't stand not knowing where you were sneaking off to. But we kept our distance."

Having these two sneak up on him made him feel ridiculous. If they discovered why he was here they would never let him hear the end of it.

Of course, neither would they let him hear the end of it if he backed off now. They would harp at him until they found out whose house this was, and why he had almost gone in but hadn't. Word would spread. Reasons would be invented. He'd be the laughing stock of Portuguese Creek and beyond.

Without explaining anything, he said, "Wait here," and stepped out of the hearse to walk up the cracked concrete walkway to the wooden steps, and then up the steps to the front door. He looked back to make sure that Peterson had got back inside the Henry J with Cynthia. Then, aware he was holding his breath, he pushed the buzzer. After a second buzz, the door was opened by a woman in a flowered blouse and striped bib-apron, holding a feather duster in one hand. She was not the woman at last night's concert. Her white hair was so sparse he could see a good deal of scalp.

Of course he remembered that Myrtle's father had kept a housekeeper. Myrtle had believed he would eventually marry her.

"That was quick!" the woman said, squinting in the direction of the hearse. Then, instead of asking him who he was or why he'd rung the bell, she turned immediately away and started down the narrow hallway.

He could follow or he could stand here looking the fool.

There'd been some sort of mistake of course, but he had not been given a chance to explain himself, or to ask for the lady of the house. Should he stand where he was until she came back to ask him his business?

But she had stopped at an open doorway and looked back. "Well?" As though he'd been expected and should know what to do.

He couldn't think of how to explain himself with this distance between them. Yet, when he stepped in and started down the hall, already beginning to explain, to tell her his name at least, she shook her head to silence him, and indicated that he should go before her through the open door.

This was a small bedroom — dark, the curtains closed. A white sheet had been pulled up over a figure laid out on a narrow bed.

"You've brought a casket?" the woman said.

"A casket?" Arvo said. He had brought Henderson's coffin, of course, but why would she want to know this?

A dangerous stew of anger and disappointment and regret had begun to boil up in his chest. Stupid damn idiot! He had left it too late. Not even time to say goodbye, or to let her know that he'd thought about her often all these years.

He removed his cap. "Is this *her*?" He could not bear to say her name. And he was not about to turn back the sheet. He turned away — he would not have this woman notice his eyes were wet.

"Of course it's her," the old woman said. "Are your helpers not bringing a casket in ... ?"

When he said nothing, she raised her voice as though he might not have heard. "I was expecting Ben Robinson to come for her himself."

This was said like an accusation, as though he had ignored instructions. "You can't have worked for him long, I think, or . . ."

"I'm sorry," Arvo said, turning away and heading back down the hallway towards the front door. "There's been a mistake."

He went out and down the steps, aware that the woman followed, calling "Wait! I don't understand."

When he turned back to attempt an explanation, another woman had appeared beside her in the doorway. "Good heavens," this second woman said. She left the other in the doorway and followed him down the steps and the short cracked concrete path to the sidewalk where she hurried ahead of him with the long fast steps of someone determined to straighten things out. "That's not Ben Robinson's hearse!"

Before Arvo could offer an explanation, she gasped. "Where on earth did he find this?"

She brushed past him to cross the street, then placed a hand against the nearest head lamp. "This is exactly like a hearse my father once owned." She turned to him, smiling. "Oh, it's typical of Ben to go to the trouble of finding this, to take dear Isabel away in the style she deserves."

The name "Isabel" did not mean anything to Arvo. He was more interested in observing this woman's face, in listening to the familiarity in her voice.

"My cousin," she explained, "who has shared this old house with me for more than thirty years."

The woman with the duster had disappeared from the doorway.

Arvo felt a surge of relief. Not only was the deceased woman not Myrtle, he could see, now, that this tall woman who had come out and down the steps was Charlie Birdsong's daughter. While the years had not preserved her girlhood beauty, or even the mature good looks of the woman who'd attended that funeral years ago, this did not prevent him from seeing something of the girl who had grown to possess this woman's older body without losing the sparkle in her eyes.

But now that sparkle was replaced by something like indignation. "This is *it*, isn't it! My father's. Where have you kept it all this time?" Myrtle Birdsong appeared to be trying to contain her outrage. "Why are you here with it now?"

"Myrtle," he said, "I . . ." But saw that she'd flinched at this intimacy. "I drove the whole of yesterday in order to bring this home to you. Does that sound like a thief's behaviour?" This was not how he'd imagined things. "I don't know who had it all this time. I've only had it long enough to fix it up and drive it down."

She leaned close to lift his mother's blanket from the driver's seat and examine the weather-damaged material beneath it. She frowned at the instrument panel, perhaps noticing scratches that would not have drawn themselves to his attention. "And how did you know where to bring it?" She turned then for the first time to look directly at him.

"I remember the neighbourhood, I remember the house. I could tell you where the piano used to sit. I could tell you where we studied together once." He pointed to the farther of the two dormer windows. "A small paint-chipped wine-coloured desk."

Then he said his name.

Maybe her eyesight was poor. And it *had* been several years since she'd come north for that funeral. He reminded her that he'd turned the pages of her music whenever she played the piano in public. Before his parents moved him away.

"Yes yes," she said. "Of course!" But still she frowned. Then it seemed she remembered, or thought she remembered. "Arvo? You made sure my science experiments were tidied up before the teacher saw my mess."

He told her about rescuing the hearse from a family of loggers in the mountains and travelling all this distance to collect a dear friend and give him a friendly send-off that did not depend upon the usual professional folks who would take all the intimacy out of a funeral. "And then, once we've done that, to return it to you. I guess I should have waited until after all that before coming here but I . . ."

She did not wait for that sentence to end. "You'll bury your friend here? In the city?"

"Oh no," he said. "We'll take him home."

He was a fool! He should have waited until after Martin's funeral to show her the hearse. If he had mentioned to Peterson or Cynthia what he was up to they would have warned him not to bring it here this morning. He was like the child who couldn't wait. Who acted before thinking. He'd wanted the pleasure of seeing her gratitude, and now he had probably lost the opportunity to take Martin home in this hearse. Myrtle Birdsong would insist on taking possession of it immediately.

"Well look!" she exclaimed, putting a hand against a glass panel. "All these flowers inside! How beautiful! Hundreds of them in bloom!"

It was true. It seemed the morning sunlight had encouraged the flowers to open in just the past few minutes. A great crowd of large white blooms filled all the space between the glass and the casket.

It seemed only natural to open the rear door and remove the closest pot. "Since you've had a death too, and will probably have company arriving."

She smiled and accepted the flowers and bent to breathe their scent. Then she took a step back in order to study him better, half-closing her eyes. "Your pale hair has thinned out, but I certainly know those blue Finnish eyes. And the cheekbones. But just to be sure, show me your hands." She shifted the potted plant to the crook of one arm and took his right hand in hers and turned it palms-up. "Even so, I remember noticing at that funeral," she said. "You worked with engines. You'd probably scrubbed yourself raw before leaving home, but I remember reading your future in those lines that no amount of scrubbing could remove. I remember wondering what those lines might have told me, but of course I didn't suspect *this!*" Her gesture seemed to imply that *this* was today, these flowers, the hearse, everything that was happening now or might yet happen.

They had never held hands as youngsters. He remembered wondering if it might be possible. But he hadn't dared, knowing he could risk losing the chance to be the one who helped. There were others who could have replaced him if she'd sent him packing — by her, or by her father.

The long sleek modern hearse pulling up behind the Henry J was nearly silent, a purring giant compared to the Cadillac Cathedral. Did modern corpses require twice the space and five times the amount of steel to protect them from the world, and several times the horsepower in order to haul all that extra amount of steel at a turtle's pace?

Ben Robinson — if this was Ben Robinson who stepped out from behind the wheel — was a young man. Too young, Arvo thought, for such a sober business. He would be cynical by thirty-five. He'd arrived in shirtsleeves to collect the body, probably convinced that informality made people more comfortable with someone in his business.

His helper was even younger, if this was possible — a boy who looked so pleased with himself he must think he'd landed the world's best summer holiday job.

But the driver was obviously annoyed to be confronted with this surprise. "What's this?" he said. "*What's this?*" He could have meant "What's this piece of junk parked in my way?" or "What's this trick you've played on me?"

"Ben!" Myrtle Birdsong stepped forward, smiling, to greet him. A *strained* sort of smile, it seemed to Arvo. "It was my father's — look! From long ago!"

When those of us who are now old were still young.

The youthful driver circled the Cathedral hearse with the look of a man who hoped to find a reason to have it hauled away. Of course he would not have to think long. He could ask for ownership papers. He could phone the competition bureau to make a complaint. He would not accuse Myrtle Birdsong of betraying him but would put all of the blame on this lanky old man with the thinning hair and the "Finnish eyes."

These possibilities may have occurred to her as well. "Don't you find it beautiful?" she said. "This gentleman has brought it home."

"But not for today," Arvo quickly added. She had misunderstood — his fault. "I'll bring it down again the minute we've taken our friend home for a proper send-off. I just wanted you to see that it was safe and in good working order."

"Of course," she said. "But please wait . . ." She barely touched his shirt sleeve. "Wait till Ben has taken Isabel away. Maybe you and your friends in that strange-looking car could come inside for a cup of tea? No, I expect you'd choose coffee, like every Finn I've ever known. Sucking it through a sugar cube between your front teeth." She laughed.

"Not me," Peterson said, when Arvo had relayed the invitation. "I've gotta get back. Lucy will destroy me if she wakes up and thinks I've run out on her."

Of course Cynthia chose this moment to step out of the Henry J. She'd waited this long, he supposed, to see what his plans were — though it was not like Cynthia to be shy. But neither would it be like Cynthia to resent his giving one pot of her flowers to a woman who had just lost a cousin. "You should use the phone while you're inside," she said to Arvo. "Let the hospital know we'll be by to pick up Martin. We'll wait."

CHAPTER 13

⚭

WHILE HE WAITED FOR someone at the hospital to pick up the phone, he watched from the central hallway as Myrtle Birdsong brought solemn-looking visitors into the living room, most of them of her generation, and his. Her relatives, he guessed, or friends of the deceased cousin. More women than men, which seemed to be the situation everywhere now, at least amongst people his age.

Like Myrtle, these people appeared to be saddened but not devastated. The death may have been long in coming. No one here wore black. Myrtle's dress was a sort of light beige, with short sleeves and a skirt that shifted around the hem as she moved. Something a tall woman would probably feel comfortable in. It looked expensive to him, but of course he had no idea what women paid for their clothes.

The house smelled of furniture polish, just as he remembered it smelling when he'd come by with classmates to practise for a school concert or work on a group science project. Or had come alone to help with her homework. Maybe his coming alone had not happened quite as often as he'd thought — certainly not so often that she'd remembered immediately once he'd brought it up.

Myrtle, he could see, was gracious, graceful, soft-spoken — more or less as he'd imagined. She'd become a rather "stately" woman, yet quick to smile as though she genuinely liked whoever she was speaking to. Maybe she did like everyone who hadn't given her a reason not to.

When someone finally responded to the ringing phone, he identified himself and said he'd be there very soon to pick up Martin Glass.

"You called yesterday?"

"I did."

"Well, I'm terribly sorry! But I'm afraid that when no one arrived yesterday afternoon as we'd expected, and we got no answer at your home number, we arranged for Mr. Glass's remains to be sent north to the Henderson Funeral Home first thing this morning. Of course we got in touch with Mr. Henderson, to make sure they were expecting him."

"And now?"

"Gone, I'm afraid."

Arvo replaced the phone, closed his eyes, and hauled in a long deep breath. Stupid! His stupid fault . . . assuming that Martin would wait while he satisfied his own private hopes.

So now, with a knot in his stomach, he had to ask permission to use the phone again, this time for a long-distance call to make sure that David Henderson understood there'd been no change to the original plan. "They knew we were to pick him up for you but they got impatient," he explained. "Just stick to the plan when he gets there. We want to scatter his ashes on the ocean out front of Martin's house."

"On the *ocean*?"

"Martin was always happy on the water."

"I know Martin was happy on the water but my God, Arvo, you haven't forgotten that he was a public figure? He belonged to more than just his few close friends. I thought you'd want a proper ceremony here in town — open to the public. With a grave that admirers could visit."

"The public didn't give a damn about Martin once he was out of politics. It's only his friends now, and his neighbours."

"Well . . ." Dave Henderson let a few moments of silence go by. "If you say so."

"Have you got a nice-looking pot of some kind to put him in?"

"Hell no, I was going to turn him over to you in a rusty soup can — what did you think?" He let a moment of silence go by. "I guess I can rustle up something. We've only got a few dozen choices in the storeroom. I figure Martin Glass belongs in a stainless steel cylinder, no decoration. He was a simple man."

He was not a simple man. He was a man who chose to *appear* simple. Arvo suspected this was one of Martin's techniques for achieving things without drawing too much attention to himself — a technique that had turned out to be of little use in the House of Commons. On the television you saw them baying and snarling like hounds on the scent — motivated largely by contempt for one another. Contempt as well, it seemed, for the voters who sent them there.

When he explained the changed circumstances to Myrtle she insisted he not rush away. "Stay, please, for a little visit. Invite your friends in for coffee."

Outside, Peterson was leaning against the Henry J and studying the pavement while Cynthia examined the flowering fuchsia bushes along the front edge of the Birdsong lawn. "You mean we came all the way down here for nothing?" Peterson said.

"We didn't know it would be for nothing," Arvo said. "We didn't know the damn hospital would be in such a hurry to get rid of Martin."

He took a deep breath and waited through the silence that followed.

"I guess we took longer to get here than they thought we should," Cynthia eventually suggested.

"I guess you're right," Arvo said. He resisted the urge to blame Herbie for this. "The lady has invited us in for coffee."

"Naw!" Peterson said. "I better get back to Lucy."

"I have never turned down an invitation for coffee," Cynthia said.

"Well," Peterson said. "If we make it quick."

As they were about to go up the steps, they were joined by an elderly couple who'd just stepped out of a black Mercedes. The woman introduced herself and her companion as "Birdsong cousins from Vancouver."

Coffee was served, and cake. The deceased cousin would have been flattered by the compliments Arvo overheard. It seemed she had been "selfless" and "energetic" in her service to others. And extremely generous to the homeless you saw on the streets.

The conversations had less of his attention than his memories of being in this house so long ago. Was that upright piano beneath the high window the same piano where he'd turned pages for her? It looked much as he remembered. A Heintzman. The dining-room table may not be the same table but it stood in the same spot where he'd sometimes helped her with her school projects. And the closed doors to unseen rooms reminded him now, as they had then, that this house was home to a business where her father prepared bodies for burial — though of course all that had taken place in another building.

But they could not sit here for long, making small talk with strangers. Peterson was obviously uncomfortable, edging his way towards the door. Cynthia raised her eyebrows as though expecting some sort of instruction from Arvo. Since Myrtle was busy being a hostess, she could pay little attention to him aside from the occasional smile — perhaps a conspiratorial smile — as she passed by with the coffee pot or a tray of cakes, or turned from welcoming newcomers into the room

"Time for us to move on," he said, getting to his feet the next time she glanced his way. He offered a hand for Myrtle to shake, but she clasped it in her own and did not let go while she walked him out onto the veranda. "Thank you for thinking of me," she said. "This is a day when the arrival of an old friend is certainly appreciated. I can imagine Cousin Isabel smiling if she had known."

"But she wouldn't know who I was."

She smiled and squeezed his hand. "Perhaps. Perhaps not."

Now that they had come to this moment, he took a deep breath and made what felt like a serious plunge. "If you came up to join us next Saturday you'd see your father's hearse put to good use again. I could even tell you something of its history since you saw it last. Then we can bring it back here and do whatever you want with it."

"It will make for a sad week," she said, looking off down the street. "One funeral after another." For a moment she examined a potted geranium on the veranda ledge and removed a dying leaf.

By the time she'd released his hand so that he could go down the steps, Cynthia had gone ahead to open the rear door of the hearse and bring out another pot of her blooming flowers, and then a second, and carried them — one in each arm — up to present them to Myrtle. To Arvo she said. "Will you help?"

Of course he knew what she meant. He joined Peterson to remove more of Cynthia's potted flowers from the hearse and carry them up to the house. "I'm sure these will be happy here," Cynthia said to Arvo when she'd returned for a second load, then lowered her voice to add, "Let her family see that country hicks sometimes know how to behave."

After carrying the last of the flowers inside, Arvo found Myrtle refilling a coffee pot in the kitchen, and offered to return to discuss the hearse once the guests had gone. She put a hand on his arm and lowered her voice. "I'm afraid not all of them will be going anywhere. The Vancouver cousins will be staying for a few days. And a niece." She glanced at her wrist. "And immediately after lunch I must rush off to the university for a board meeting, which I've been promised will be brief."

"You're on the Board of Directors?"

She laughed. "Oh dear, no. My father left a generous amount to a certain renewable fund and I am invited to take his place at their meetings. I'm sorry. It meets so infrequently that not even today is a good enough excuse to stay away."

"Then I'll see you when I return the hearse. Naturally it should still belong to you. We'll dig up a lawyer and make sure it does. Of course you could decide to come up for Martin's funeral and bring it home yourself. "

She studied her own hand for a moment, opening and closing her fingers. Then said, without looking up, "It would be lovely to see you, of course. But I'm sorry, I have to tell you that I really think I would rather not have the hearse returned, despite the pleasure of discovering it has been so well cared for."

Arvo was not sure he knew what she meant. "After your cousin's funeral then?"

"No-no. I meant I would rather you found something else to do with it — donate it to a museum, sell it to a vintage car collector, drive it off a cliff. Well!" She laughed. "I didn't mean with you in it. If there is a way of keeping it safe somewhere, then please do — but I would rather not have it returned."

Of course he'd known there was a possibility of this. "But it was your father's."

"Exactly," she said, and held out her arms for Cynthia to pass over another pot of flowers. "These are lovely, lovely!" She put them down on the nearest table and turned again to Arvo, laying her hand lightly on his arm. "I'm sorry. It was a lovely idea, but I just couldn't . . ."

It seemed that he was supposed to imagine the rest. "Couldn't" rather than "wouldn't" or "shouldn't." There were things he didn't know. About the father, or about the brief unsatisfactory husband who had driven the hearse for a while.

When the flowers had all been delivered inside, Peterson announced that he ought to get a move-on, in case Lucy was fed up with waiting. "She'll have found out about another shopping mall she wants me to take her to, I can tell you that. She hardly ever gets away from her chickens. And she won't be very much fun to be with if she's forced to leave early."

"Well then," Arvo said. "Some of us will have to set off without her. You can decide for yourself if you'll wait. While you're at it, you can think about stopping in to visit Herbie on your way home."

"Hell, I wouldn't even know where to look."

"I'll leave directions at the motel desk if I check out before you're back from your spree. Cynthia's Honda will have to be my Escort Car going home."

Cynthia decided to ride back to the motel with him in the hearse. To Arvo she said, "I want you to show me your old neighbourhood." There was something in her voice that made him wonder how much she'd guessed of his reason for coming here. She'd been a teacher after all, with that teacher's talent for reading your mind.

Once she'd got in to sit beside him he could sense without looking that she was smiling up at him, so he turned to see if she was serious about a tour. She was, though her bright clever eyes shone with some other sort of mischief. "Take us past your house. Show me your school. Point out where you held hands with Myrtle for the first time — since I can't believe that you didn't. She must have been very beautiful."

"Good grief!" This had escaped before he could stop it. Did she have no idea that he felt like a bloody fool right now?

Still, he started the hearse and drove out to the first major street and turned in the direction that would take them through his old neighbourhood. "I didn't mean to shout," he said. "All that back there was hard."

"Maybe you should go back later," Cynthia suggested. "After the guests have gone."

Arvo stared straight ahead. What had she noticed? Or, what did she think she'd noticed? It was stupid, of course, but he could imagine the people in Myrtle's living room having a chuckle at his expense. To Myrtle it must have seemed that he'd behaved like a teen-aged boy trying to impress the class beauty.

Cynthia had asked where he'd first held Myrtle's hand. Was it true that he never really held her hand? It seemed improbable now, but yes, he supposed there was the once. "Of course it was an accident," he said. "Taking her hand, I mean. And it didn't last very long. Everybody knew her father would nail you up in a coffin if you paid too much attention to his daughter. If you were caught."

"So you were careful not to hold hands near her house."

"We were careful not to hold hands at all after that first time. They said that if the old man ever let you out of the coffin it would be only so he could take a butcher knife to your . . . you know."

"Oh dear." Cynthia shuddered dramatically. "And there was no mother to show him what a fool he was?"

He would make her tour a quick one. He was in no mood to be a tour guide. At the moment he could imagine himself as a tourist-attraction. *This here is a statue of an old man who made a fool of himself trying to impress the girl he'd been sort of in love with more than sixty years in the past. It is now a local tradition to throw eggs, aiming especially for the face.*

An alley took them directly from Myrtle's neighbourhood to the street where his family home had once stood. A furniture warehouse took up the whole block now — all houses demolished, or moved away. Strange that this didn't bother him. It was almost as though he was glad this had happened. Something that belonged entirely in your past might as well disappear altogether once you were no longer part of it. Otherwise, things could get confusing.

Egg on his face. At least Peterson knew nothing about all this. He *hoped* Peterson hadn't heard about any of it. If Peterson knew, he wasn't likely to keep quiet about it. And if he did keep quiet it would be from pity — which would be almost as bad as mockery, or gossip.

The school in the next block had not disappeared but it had been renovated so extensively there was nothing left he could recognize. "This cemetery up ahead could be the only thing that hadn't changed in this part of the city. The residents could not be bribed to move on."

A stone wall bordered the road as far as the entrance, which was barred by an ironwork gate. Leafy trees and tall stone monuments were all that could be seen beyond it. "We used to play cops and robbers in there. Cowboys and Indians. Hide and Seek. Whatever we wanted."

"They're an unfriendly selfish bunch, the dead," Cynthia said. "Keeping this lovely property to themselves. I'm glad you brought a little life to it for a while."

The road carried them past the field where Arvo had played football. "I was pretty good at it. Soccer they call it now." Then it curved to join a road that followed the coastline. Directly below was the sandy cove where he sometimes swam, or sometimes just turned over rocks to study the strange colourful life of the startled sea creatures beneath. "Myrtle was not allowed anywhere near this." A little farther along, in a field of grass between road and cliff-edge, was the pond where he'd once sailed his miniature boats. "She did join me here — just once — but reached too far out and fell in. Went home drenched."

"You went with her, to help her face the music."

"She wouldn't let me. In her old man's eyes I would've been worse news than a drowning. Growing up without a mother must be tough."

Of course none of these places had any magic in them now. He'd stayed clear of this in all the years since, suspecting they would only disappoint.

He was no longer sure he knew what he wanted for himself. Throughout the whole process of rescuing the hearse, preparing it for the journey, driving it south, and delivering it to her doorstep, he had had his doubts but had never seriously believed she might not want it back. He must have been wearing some sort of blinkers, like the horses that pulled funeral carriages in the old days.

Well, he did know he was pleased to have seen her. Seeing her again was what he had wanted, after all — though his foolish imagination had insisted on hoping for more.

When they came to a small coffee shop perched above the water's edge, a white cruise ship several storeys high and the length of two city blocks was slowly nudging its way into place alongside a long concrete dock. Cynthia put a hand on his arm and asked him to stop. "The world has come to our doorstep," she said.

He pulled in to the curb where it was possible to see the full length of the ship, including the blunt front end that made it look more like a five-storey floating hotel than an old-time pointed-nose ocean liner.

"I've always wanted to sail off on one of those," Cynthia said. "To Hawaii or maybe New Zealand. But I suspect it will never happen. Right now I just want to watch the lucky ones get off. I don't suppose you want me to go in and bring us out some coffee."

"No more coffee!" Arvo said.

They sat in silence to watch the activity around the cruise ship.

Of course he couldn't help but relive his last few minutes with Myrtle. "I suppose I made a damn fool of myself this morning," he eventually said. "After making this whole stupid trip."

"Well maybe." Cynthia sounded rather cheerful about this. "But frankly, it was about time. I was beginning to believe you'd live to a hundred and still be the only person in the world who hasn't made a fool of himself at least once."

There wasn't much he could say to that, beyond a sort of growl. He knew there were some who believed he made a fool of himself every day he spent in his workshop, while everyone else his age was flying off to lie on Hawaiian beaches or climb the Italian Alps.

"Well I was wrong," Cynthia added. "There was the once."

He knew what she meant. "The woman from Thunder Bay?"

"Though frankly I thought you handled it rather well in the end. Henry said he would have shot her if he'd been you." She waited a moment before adding "Of course I don't imagine he meant it."

Cynthia's husband had said a lot of things he didn't mean — in order to raise a few eyebrows or just get a laugh.

"You think pushing a kicking screaming woman onto the bus was handling it well?"

"It was a lot more civilized than what I would have done."

It wasn't long before people began to pour out of the cruise ship

— an apparently endless swarm spilling out from some discreetly tucked-away exit in the hull, many of them rushing immediately out across the pavement towards the waiting buses and taxis. Still, a good number of them seemed to be content to stand around and take in their new location: the coastline, the harbour, the city centre at the head of the harbour.

"Those people pouring out of that boat remind me of a book I read," Arvo said. "A long time ago now. Only it was the reverse — sentence after sentence describing hordes of pilgrims pouring down out of the world to get onto the rusty old ship that they didn't know would later start to sink and threaten to drown them. I still have my copy somewhere."

"Joseph Conrad," Cynthia said. "I read it too, but long ago. That parade of doomed pilgrims is the one thing that stuck in my mind."

"My old man came to this country working on a rusty freighter expecting every minute to be told they were sinking. I told him he ought to read the book, but of course he never did, he just asked me for a quick report."

"A good story," Cynthia the former teacher said. "But with very long sentences."

"I was tempted to read it aloud so maybe when I got to the end of each sentence I might have a chance of remembering how it started."

"Well," Cynthia said — cheerfully, he thought — "I hope it wasn't the only book you read in your whole long life."

He said nothing to this. Of course she had to be aware of the James Lee Burke novels on his workbench. She would not have recommended Burke to her high-school English students — or to him either, if she'd known that in every one of them the likeable detective was faced with the most vicious brand of murderers a human mind could possibly dream up.

Some of the tourists had come up onto the roadside pavement on foot, apparently not interested in the tour buses that would have taken them to shops where they could part with their money. Soon it was clear that a crowd had begun to gather around the hearse: Asian faces, though Arvo couldn't guess what country they may have been from. It was also impossible to know what they were saying to one another — a language unlike any he had ever heard. Maybe they were trying to decide if they were looking at the usual form of transportation in this country. Maybe they believed this was one of the "tourist attractions" they'd been promised. Were they looking for someone to sell them tickets for a ride?

"Hearse!" Arvo said, getting out to stand beside his open door. "For funerals!"

The nearest man, grinning, rushed forward to take hold of his hand and pump it enthusiastically a few times, but his words might have been lines from some foreign opera. The others, frowning, watched this. Wondering, maybe, if they were expected to shake his hand as well.

He had no other words to explain this vehicle to them, but Cynthia got out and took up the challenge. "For the dead!" she shouted, tapping at the nearest window — presumably to draw attention to the coffin inside. She closed her eyes, let her tongue hang out one corner of her mouth, crossed her arms against her breast, and let her head drop to the side like someone shot.

"Awwwwww!" Some of the tourists nodded solemnly, though others appeared even more puzzled than before. Then, suddenly, all of them turned away to see what other wonders might be found in this foreign place. Some of the couples walked down the trail towards the coffee shop.

"Well!" Arvo said, once Cynthia had got in again beside him. "For a minute there I thought you were going to crawl in the back and play dead for them!"

"It crossed my mind. But I was afraid you'd drive off and make me ride in there all the way to the motel!"

"It would serve you right."

"Of course you wouldn't get away with it, because I'd push my face against the glass and hammer my fists and scream for help from the people out on the sidewalks! You'd end up explaining yourself to police."

After a few moments of silence she added: "Well now, before we return to Real Life, I'd be very interested in meeting some of those tourists who went inside. What do you think? Do you have room for another coffee, or a piece of pie? I've always wondered what it would be like to travel the world on a ship."

"I suppose I could watch you drink a coffee but I won't have any myself. I don't want to stop for a pee every hour the whole way home."

"That shouldn't be a problem. This contraption goes slow enough. You could jump off, leaving it to putter on ahead, find a tree to pee behind, and catch up before it's gone more than a dozen metres up the road."

"You give me too much credit," he said. "Some things just aren't as fast as they used to be." Then, in case she misunderstood. "I meant, these legs aren't too keen on running."

Cynthia laughed. "I notice most of those tourists are getting on in age, so I imagine the cruise ships have plenty of restrooms. You wouldn't have to run very far."

"I didn't say anything about taking a cruise," Arvo said.

"Not yet," she said. "But we still haven't talked to any of those folks who could tell us what it's like. Now that we've pried you this far out of your workshop there's no telling how much farther you might be tempted. Myself, I'd rather like to see Peru. Or maybe the Blue Mountains in New South Wales."

"Ha!" Arvo said. "I wanted to see Australia once but I was told it's dangerous to go there past a certain age — it would only make you depressed you aren't still thirty so you could start your life all over again down there."

"Haven't you noticed?" Cynthia said. "We start life over again every day. All of us. Even a man who hides in his workshop with grease up to his elbows. I bet the tour-bus drivers in Peru would be grateful to have you aboard when we break down halfway up one of their terrible mountains."

CHAPTER 14

❦

NEITHER ARVO NOR ANYONE else in Portuguese Creek knew whether Martin would have wanted a modest local funeral or the ceremonious sort of event his fellow parliamentarians in Ottawa might have planned if they'd still regarded him as a colleague. But Martin's friends could give him only the sort of funeral that felt both natural to them and faithful to their memories of Martin. This began with a decision not to consult with Ottawa or the local branch of Martin's political party. The fact that no one from either the party headquarters or the local branch had written an appreciation for the local paper, or a brief letter to the editor, or even contacted Martin's friends to ask about funeral plans, suggested that he had been pretty well forgotten by his former colleagues.

Arvo's arrangement with Henderson's funeral establishment allowed David Henderson to cremate the body according to legal requirements and then to drive up to Portuguese Creek and turn the ashes over to Arvo at his workshop. Nothing more. That was to be the end of officialdom's role in the death of Martin Glass.

So far as Arvo was concerned, once he and the Cadillac hearse had delivered the cylinder of ashes to Martin's house at the end of Stevenson Road, whatever else might happen was to be left to those friends and neighbours who chose to attend. They had known Martin best, and they had united to contribute a sizable number of the votes that had sent him to represent the entire valley in the national parliament.

Arvo had arranged for an item in the valley weekly to make it clear that anyone who remembered Martin with respect or affection was welcome to attend the modest event at Martin's seaside home. Of course he knew that nothing would prevent the merely curious from following Henderson's long, sleek, modern hearse down the main street of town, across the river bridge, and then north on the Old Highway as far as Portuguese Creek and Arvo's workshop, so they might as well know they'd be welcome to follow Martin the rest of the way as well — down Stevenson Road to Martin's house on the water's edge.

Myrtle Birdsong hadn't promised to attend. She hadn't shown up the evening before, and hadn't phoned this morning to say she was on her way. Of course she had not given him reason to expect her, but he'd hoped she might reconsider, in order to witness her father's hearse once more in action.

While they waited for Henderson to deliver the urn, Bert Peterson and Herbie Brewer joined Arvo in his workshop where the hearse, gleaming from a fresh wash and a wax job, sat waiting for its return to active duty. Each of them wore a white dress shirt with the top button undone, and had stuffed a rolled-up tie in a pocket just in case they were later made to feel that a tie was expected even at the beach. In the meantime they would put off for as long as possible the sensation of being strangled.

Herbie had stepped down off a coach-lines bus this morning, frowning hard. He'd come, he said, not just to attend the funeral but to claim the rest of his belongings. Once he learned that Lucy had returned to her chicken ranch rather than stay for the funeral, he agreed to spend the night at Peterson's and catch the morning bus south. He made this sound like a big concession to Peterson.

Arvo had brought out three vinyl kitchen chairs so that he and Peterson and Herbie would not have to sit on overturned oil cans or an old CIL box while they waited. But Herbie chose to stand in the open doorway so he could be the first to witness the arrival of Martin's urn.

"You hear anything from that city woman you looked up?" Peterson said. He kept his face turned away, as though he wasn't sure this was a safe question to ask. "Since we got back, I mean."

Arvo shrugged, to suggest indifference. "I thought she might want to see her old man's hearse in action, but maybe not."

"She should damn-well want to check out the man that rescued it and brought it to her too," Peterson said. "She looked pleased enough to see you on her doorstep. If she shows up you make sure you take her inside your house. Once she gets a look at them shiny floors and perfect rooms she'll beg you to let her stay — a house with its own perfect housekeeper of the male species."

When Arvo growled and frowned and turned away to tidy the tools on his workbench, Peterson added: "You forget I was inside once? If any woman gets to see what I seen, you'll be dragged down the aisle with a blue ribbon hanging from your neck. She'd think a man who keeps a house that perfect would probably cook her meals and wash her hair and even cut her toenails for her. Don't let Lucy inside or you'll have her on your hands for good. She *hates* housework."

"I'll never try to steal Lucy from you," Arvo said. "I'm pretty sure I can promise you that."

"They're here!" Herbie shouted.

Peterson and Arvo joined Herbie at the doorway to watch Henderson's sleek hearse turn off the Highway and pull up in front of the shop. David Henderson got out from behind the wheel and went back to open the rear door and remove the urn. Apparently it had not travelled on the seat beside Henderson as you might have expected of something hardly larger than a milk carton, but had made the journey where a casket would have sat if there had been one.

"Here you go," Henderson said, handing the cylinder to Arvo. "Martin Glass himself. Well, he's not exactly 'himself,' but I take it this is what you're waiting for."

Then, before turning back to his hearse, he said he would stay here and take up the rear of the procession. "Having had my hand in this business, so to speak, I'd like to see 'er through to the end."

Before crossing the highway to start down Stevenson Road, Arvo could see that a long column of cars had either followed Martin from town or joined the parade somewhere along the way — all waiting now alongside the pavement for him and the Cathedral hearse to take the lead for this final stage of the journey. Martin would be pleased to see that some trucks were pulling boats on their trailers. Being something of a fisherman himself, he'd always enjoyed seeing boats on the water. Because Martin's place was on the water's edge, some naturally assumed the funeral celebration would be an opportunity to sail, or to water ski, maybe even to put a line in the water for an extra salmon to wrap in foil for the barbecue. Ed Forrester was fourth down the row, with his twenty-foot catamaran behind his truck. Mario Lopez's SUV was pulling his brand new speedboat on its yellow trailer. And the Young family had a small rowboat in the bed of their pickup truck — a GMC from the fifties that Arvo had rescued from the bush out behind Woodsons' sawmill.

Martin would be happy to see that people were planning to take advantage of the usually calm water in his protected bay. He'd kept a small boat himself, as well as a canoe for exploring the nearby coves and inlets up and down the coast. Occasionally he'd dropped a line in the water just to see if anything would bite, and invited friends to come down for a meal whenever he'd caught and baked a salmon of a decent size.

As soon as the Cathedral hearse started across the highway with Peterson's Henry J behind it, drivers who'd stood talking on the roadside grass hurried back to their vehicles. Doors slammed shut all down the row. The first few cars and trucks began to move up, ready to follow down the narrow road to the beach.

For a while Arvo led the way alongside property where Cynthia and her husband had operated their drive-in movie theatre on weekends. The field was overgrown with scrub willows and alder whose summer foliage made it impossible to see what was left of the wooden frame behind the long-disappeared screen. Henry and Cynthia had talked him into driving down to see Jane Wyman and Rock Hudson in *Magnificent Obsession* many decades ago. Also, much later, *Cannery Row*, which may have been one of the last movies before they closed down the business and let the bush grow up through the abandoned gravel and narrow strips of pavement.

Cynthia was standing outside her gate. When Arvo got close enough, she stuck out the thumb of one hand while lifting a leg of her white slacks to show him one slim calf and ankle.

Arvo stopped beside her. "That's not a bad-looking ankle you've got on offer there, but I have to tell you I've got two of my own already. Is there something about it you wanted me to notice, or is it just that the Honda has let you down?"

She climbed in beside him to sit on his mother's row of little Suomi trees. "I delivered a carload of flowers down to Martin's place this morning and got myself stuck in the sand! I could kick myself. Had to walk home. I wasn't looking forward to walking all the way back. Let's go. I always wondered what it feels like to drive dead people around."

Arvo imagined that not too many people spent time wondering about such things. "Quieter than teaching a classroom full of teens, I'd guess."

"But not as much fun." She hummed a moment, then added, "You know, Arvo, I miss them. The students, I mean. When I see one of them in town, or up in the Store, I feel a little sorry they had to grow up. I really enjoyed them when they were teens, though you might be surprised to hear that."

"They might be a little surprised to hear that themselves. I imagine they'd also be a little shocked to see you showing off your naked ankle back there, hustling for a ride from the first man that came along."

"There's probably a few of them behind us — middle-aged by now, mostly overweight, all asking each other if that was really me climbing into the hearse and how come I wasn't dead yet. If they're shocked that I'm alive you can imagine what they'd think if they knew what I have up my sleeve."

Arvo was not anxious to hear what she had up her sleeve, but of course he had little choice. And there was a chance he might find it entertaining

"You don't plan to go back to the classroom."

"Be serious. They wouldn't let me anywhere near a classroom now, you know that. But I think I might have mentioned thinking about re-opening the drive-in."

"In all that grown-back *forest?* I thought you would've come to your senses by now."

"Bulldozers'll make quick work of that. I could have the place cleaned out in a week. Paved over soon afterward."

Arvo felt a little dizzy. It took some effort to shift his thoughts away from Martin — riding right behind him in a cylinder — to fully take in Cynthia's plans. Had no one ever told her that most people over seventy took it easy?

Of course she would consider him a poor example.

Arvo had now and then stopped on his way home from visiting Peterson or Martin Glass to watch a few minutes of a movie from behind his steering wheel while parked on the side of the road — distracted by an urge to lip-read conversations happening on the screen. *From Here to Eternity. Giant.* According to Cynthia, cars had been crammed with high-school students for the James Dean movies. She'd neither confirmed nor denied a rumour claiming she'd handed out free passes to every student driving a car with more than four paying customers in it.

Cynthia's concession booth had been dismantled years ago by vandals salvaging the lumber for their own purposes, leaving nothing but the concrete blocks the small building had rested upon. It was here, for several years, even while she was still teaching high-school English, that Cynthia had sold her home-brewed coffee, home-baked brownies, and home-made buttered popcorn on weekend evenings. She claimed not to be doing it for the money but to enjoy this convenient way of feeding her appetite for Hollywood movies at no cost to herself. She'd arranged to have a speaker installed in her booth "so the customers could come back for more of my brownies without missing a word." When her own students approached to load up on popcorn and drinks, she recognized the signals that told her when it was okay to be friendly and when it was wise to pretend she was blind to everything but their money. She'd admitted once that it nearly killed her not to warn some girls about the boys they'd come with.

Now she was planning to re-open?

"You haven't noticed there *are* no drive-in movie theatres any more? There must be a reason for it."

"Well, it'll be a novelty! *Retro*! Isn't that what they say? Of course it can't be the same as it was. Maybe we'll have to find a way to play DVDs on a gigantic TV screen."

"You going to do everything yourself? You don't have Henry to help you any more."

"I *had* noticed this, thank you. Well, I was hoping to have a word with you about that. I just didn't expect the topic to come up so soon."

"You were the one who brought it up."

"I got excited. I saw you coming down the road in this old hearse and found myself thinking a man who gets a kick out of bringing old cars back to life might like the idea of resurrecting an ancient pro-jector."

Arvo didn't quite laugh. "If you go ahead with this, what you'll want is someone handy with a computer."

"Well 'projector' was just a metaphor — a synecdoche in fact. I meant to suggest the whole shebang! A concession stand would have to be built and wired to meet the latest standards. And I'd have to put out money for new equipment."

After a few moments of silence, she suggested that once they had things up and running he might be convinced to donate a half-dozen of the most hopeless car wrecks for a permanent back row — so people without cars could come on their bikes and still have a vehicle to watch from. "We could become famous as a drive-in theatre for people who have nothing to drive."

"You could become famous as a drive-in theatre without an audience. We'll have to talk about this again."

"Well, it's your fault I even thought of it," she said. "Watching you get all those old car wrecks back on the road got me thinking."

First she had imagined them going on a cruise. Now she wanted him to help her rebuild the drive-in theatre. Was she serious about either of these? What he needed was to come up with something himself that he could imagine agreeing to.

Once they'd passed beyond Peterson's fields and barn and two-storey house flanked by a pair of flowering hawthorns, and then his back acres of second-growth fir, a long cleared field made it possible to see a wide expanse of the blue Strait and the mainland mountains beyond. Far out, a white ship moved almost imperceptibly north.

"Could be that same cruise ship we saw the other day. I've been wondering ever since," Cynthia said.

"Wondering what? If you want to go on a cruise, you should just go on a cruise. This time of year we'll see three or four going past out there every week."

"Not alone I wouldn't. I could handle a classroom full of rowdy adolescents by myself, no problem, but being alone in a crowd of foreigners would be so confusing I'd end up lost inside the first pyramid they took me to."

Arvo knew that Henry had never wanted to travel. Maybe this was because he too was convinced that Cynthia would get lost in the first pyramid they visited.

"We could try a short one first," she said. Maybe she imagined he'd said something he hadn't. "That one out there is probably on its way to Alaska. Or we could be brave and try the Caribbean, or Turkey. After spending time in Turkey, I can imagine a person would be open to all sorts of changes in their lives."

She wanted him to help rebuild her drive-in theatre, she wanted him to go travelling with her. What would she come up with next? Sooner or later she was bound to think of something he couldn't resist.

Soon they arrived at the top of the cliff that fell abruptly away to a narrow strip of land along the coastline below. The water was fairly calm, he was glad to see, though of course there were waves — shallow waves. Being out in a smallish boat had never been one of his favourite activities, but some time this afternoon he would be out there in Ed's catamaran to sprinkle Martin's ashes while the others watched from the shore or from their own boats. There was bound to be at least some breeze, so he'd have to remember to calculate the best direction to toss the ashes in order not to have them blow back in his face. Also to stand securely in a boat that was bound to be lifting and falling as well as tilting from side to side. He wasn't likely to feel too emotional while concentrating on staying upright, blowback-free, and alive.

Martin's house and property were spread out along the rim of the bay at the foot of this steep slope that Martin had referred to as "Glass's Descent." A man who considered himself to have gone downhill in his later years, Martin had once confided to Arvo that if he spent the rest of his life down here, "having fallen this far," he'd be reminded every day that there was not much danger of slipping any farther.

"You can see my car to the left," Cynthia said. "I stupidly tried to turn around where I thought was solid ground but it turned out to be nothing but sand."

The Honda's rear was down to its axle in sand, loose gravel, and a patch of yarrow, but at least it wasn't below the high-tide line. They could wait until later to haul some planks or boards out from behind Martin's house and set them down where her tires could grab hold.

He could see that a few lawyers and realtors and retired store clerks had abandoned their Saturday afternoon on the grass of Penti Pekkanen's golf course and were already heading, with cases of beer in hand, out to the driftwood logs for the pleasure of tipping back a drink while watching the tide come in, and possibly exchanging anecdotes about Martin Glass that might or might not be accurate.

Margaret Baxter came out onto Martin's deck to flap a tea towel free of crumbs. She had dressed in her mother's old clothing, as she did for all funerals — black dress, black gloves, a black hat with a veil over her face. It was known that the Baxters never threw anything away. Margaret might be in the process of setting herself up as a sort of hostess here, probably so that by the end of this event there would be more than a few people suspecting she'd had a long secret affair with Martin Glass right under their noses.

Of course it was possible she *had*. But unlikely. Martin had never said anything to make you think this was possible.

Frank and Evie Walker had driven down earlier to tidy up the house interior and help Leena Pekkinen and Margaret Baxter with the food. The Walkers' Corolla was parked on the grass to one side, at the foot of the sidelong slope of driveway, but an unfamiliar silver Mercedes convertible sat up closer to the small cedar-shake house. When Arvo had eased the hearse most of the way down the slope, Frank stepped out from the bushes with his arms out wide to stop him. "The son," he leaned down to tell Arvo. "Already here with a couple of friends. Well, he said they were friends but they look more like business partners to me. White shirts, sleeves rolled up? One of them was out there pacing off the waterfront. How many lots you think they can get outa this?"

"You told the son what we're up to?"

"I told him about scattering the ashes but I didn't tell him we'd planned to be here for the day and probably half the night. I don't suppose he imagined there'd be all that traffic lined up behind you."

Some of those behind him now honked their horns — part impatience, part high-spirits on a pleasant summer day with hardly a cloud in the sky and the sun shining down on the sea. They would have no idea yet that it was Martin's son who'd parked that Mercedes convertible possessively next to the house, throwing a damper over their plans unless they were determined to ignore him and make the best of the situation.

The rest of them would have to park up top on the hayfield. Arvo eased the hearse farther down and onto level ground directly behind the Mercedes.

Herbie walked down past the hearse and headed out across the driftwood sand and salt-grass to repair the storm-damage done to his "Booze Corral" — a ring of bleached driftwood logs set upright in sand, a primitive sort of jagged fortress he'd built in June for a party where he took responsibility for watching over everyone's drinks. At all community beach events Herbie stood guard over the ice chests, opening bottles or cans whenever their owners stopped by. Because he did not drink liquor he was considered the perfect bartender and often went home from these events with his pockets bulging with tips. "Your booze is always safe with Herbie," people said. "He won't touch the stuff himself, and he makes sure that no one else touches yours unless you told him otherwise."

There was no doubt that the middle-aged man who came around the end of the house with authoritative strides was the owner of the

Mercedes. "You and these others will have to turn around and leave," he said to Arvo. "This is private property."

His hair had been dyed a sort of pale orange colour.

"We know it's private property," Arvo said. "We also know whose private property it is. We have him with us."

Martin's son did not look much like Martin though he did have Martin's way of scowling at news he didn't like — had had this habit even as a boy. "What's that supposed to mean?"

"It means we've brought Martin home, just as he would've wanted. There's about a hundred of his friends lined up behind me, determined to give him a proper send-off."

He doubted the others would allow themselves to be stopped by a stranger with a German car and hair the colour of a turnip. "Tomorrow it will be between you and the lawyers," he offered. "Today it's between you and us. Maybe you weren't listening when this was all explained."

Martin's son looked out across the water for a while. Then he said, "All I heard was he was in hospital."

"But you came here instead of going to pay him a visit?"

The man's face coloured up. "I came here first because this is his home! I intended to take him a change of clothes when I drove down to see him."

"But you couldn't find his suit because we'd already put it on him rather than let him go into the furnace dressed in his paint-splashed old work pants he had on for his emergency trip to the hospital. Were your friends in dress shirts also planning to visit Martin?"

Two of those friends — both with sleeves rolled up over hairy forearms — had stepped into view at the front corner of the house. Jackets must have been tossed over a log or hung on a nail, or possibly laid out across the back seat of the Mercedes.

Again the blue sea was consulted, this time at considerable length.

You could see that Martin Glass's son was fighting to control his annoyance. He ran his fingers through his peculiar hair.

"The people behind me," Arvo said, "expect to make use of the public ocean, the public shoreline, and all those public driftwood logs below the high-tide line. Maybe Martin's covered deck too, if it rains. You and your friends will hear a good deal of noise but it will all be good-natured noise. We won't go inside your father's house without your permission."

"We'll need to use the fridge," Cynthia said, putting a hand on Arvo's arm.

"We'll need to use the fridge," Arvo said.

In his mirror he could see Peterson hurrying down the slope on foot, no doubt to find out what was going on.

"Oh, to hell with it!" said Martin Glass's son. "Go ahead and use the goddamn house. A month from now it'll be gone — towed away on a raft. There'll be *No Trespassing* signs at the top of the road, maybe coils of barbed wire if it's needed. Have your stupid picnic while you can."

"This *stupid picnic* is Martin's picnic." This was Peterson, who'd come down behind the hearse. "You can join us or you can haul your asses out of here until tomorrow."

"Take it easy," Arvo lowered his voice to say. He got out of the hearse and shut the door. "The man has already said we could use the place."

Those who had parked their vehicles at the top of the hill were now hurrying down the steep slope on foot, carrying freezer chests and shopping bags filled with bottles and beer cartons. Cynthia got out of the hearse and stood with a hand blocking the sun from her eyes while she watched the others descend.

Matthew Foreman was having some trouble navigating a safe descent, the box in his arms so big he could barely see over it, so he was likely to trip on one of the rocks that had worked their way to the surface of Martin's road. Not surprisingly, the newspaper writer was walking beside him, carrying a leather case that no doubt contained her camera and tape recorder. Even at this distance you could see she was excited to think she was about to get her story after all and wouldn't even need the co-operation of the lanky tight-mouthed old man who'd refused to have his photo taken in his ancient hearse.

Jenny Banks was in the crowd. And Mauno Pekkanen, neglecting the family golf course — his hefty sister Leena clinging to his arm in order not to break her neck on this steep slope. Arvo hoped that the wide flat box Mauno was carrying contained loaves of Leena's famous *pulla*. She would expect to be asked for the recipe fifty times before this day was through but would refuse to divulge her secrets. Of course her recipe was in Arvo's mother's recipe box and probably in any number of other recipe boxes throughout the district.

It was beginning to look as though the entire community had planned to show up. Maybe Martin had more admirers than Arvo had realized. After years of neglect he was suddenly a local hero. Or maybe curiosity had merely trumped the prospect of an afternoon mowing lawns. The gap between nosy and caring was fairly slim.

"Look," Cynthia said. "Up at the top. The white dress — *and white high heels, for heaven's sake!* — walking like she's terrified of falling. Isn't that *her* — your, you know, the woman we stopped in on?"

For a moment Arvo wasn't sure — though the white dress and white umbrella did stand out amongst the others in their beach clothes.

"Why would she want an umbrella on a sunny day?"

Cynthia had taken his hand in hers. Was this to offer him reassurance of some kind, or to seek it for herself? "That's a *parasol*," she said. "It isn't rain she's afraid of, it's the sun. She's a delicate *city* girl braced to mix with us primitives in all this rugged Nature!"

CHAPTER 15

❧

THIS WAS RIDICULOUS. No, *he* was ridiculous. As soon as he'd seen that it was Myrtle Birdsong working her way down the gravel slope of Martin's driveway, holding a parasol overhead and taking care where she put her white high-heeled shoes, he experienced a surge of anger. Or maybe it was irritation. He'd half-expected her, some part of him had even hoped to see her here — but now that she'd appeared he felt something like resentment, that she would show up unannounced so soon after turning down his offer to return her father's hearse.

Well, if she'd come to check up on it, here it was — parked to one side while neighbours hurried past. Its mission for today was over. Martin would be completing his journey by boat.

She was far too intent on watching where to put her feet to notice him. And he'd rather behave as though he'd hadn't noticed her, at least for now. Since Cynthia had gone into Martin's house to help Leena carry the food out onto the deck, Arvo set off to see if Johnny Johnson had remembered to bring his horseshoes and, if he had, to help him prepare a horseshoe pitch on the weedy grass between Martin's tool shed and his overturned skiff.

Peterson had taken the Community Association's badminton equipment out to look for a spot where wind off the sea wouldn't blow shuttlecocks into the wild-rose bushes along the base of the cliff. This reminded Arvo that later in the afternoon, either he or Peterson must relieve Herbie in the Booze Corral so that Herbie could run in for the brief swim he'd planned to honour the man who'd taught him how — though not, he'd said, if the weather turned cold. It remained to be seen if anyone would join him.

Children were already flying their colourful kites out along the water's edge. The sounds of their laughter carried, like all sounds down here, with a sort of crystal clarity. The light breeze that carried their voices also carried the fresh salt smell of the sea.

As he passed by the lower side of the house, he could smell the food Leena must have brought with her. She had probably prepared a complete *seisova poyta*, which everyone but the Finns would assume was a Swedish *smorgasbord*. Smoked salmon, salted herring. A huge bowl of cauliflower soup. Beetroot salad. Some sort of berry soup for dessert. Her donations to public events never varied.

Of course others would have brought the more common sort of summer fare that Martin had preferred — potato salad, green salads, cold ham, fried chicken.

While Margaret Baxter and Leena Pekkinen carried bowls and platters of food out onto the deck tables and covered them with tea towels against flies, a tall young woman in a long skirt sat against the wall to play her cello — a town relative of the Baxters, Arvo believed. Her music was soft, melancholy — chosen, he supposed, to suit the occasion.

"A gentleman at the General Store gave me directions," Myrtle Birdsong said, suddenly beside him. "I suppose I forgot about this gathering, or had the date wrong. I'd driven up just hoping for a chance to speak — to apologize, actually, for turning away your offer so casually. In the circumstances, I hardly knew what I was saying." She turned to look off to the sparkling water of the Strait, but tilted the parasol to keep herself in its shade.

"Well," Arvo said, "I didn't warn you I was coming. We dropped in when you were probably still in shock."

"And I did not properly express my gratitude. Or my admiration for your skill in restoring my father's dear old hearse!" She put a white-gloved hand on his arm. "If you are still willing to return it — after today, of course — I've come to thank you for it as graciously as I should have done when you showed up at my door bearing flowers."

Arvo tilted his head to view her aslant. "You're sure of this?"

She nodded, briefly closing her eyes. "Of course I don't intend to keep it to myself."

It would be absurd for her to keep the hearse, she acknowledged, since she was not a funeral director and had no intention of becoming one now. "I've spoken to Ben Robinson, who may want to use it occasionally — whenever he is given responsibility for the funeral of, say, an important politician, or a local historian or a personal friend of mine. I'm sure my father would have approved."

Ben had agreed, she said, to put the old hearse on display in some manner, so that people could admire it without doing it harm. "Behind glass, I expect."

Arvo supposed that being on display in a picture window was preferable to hauling logs in the mountains, but neither was what the hearse had been originally built for. Of course she'd said it could be used for special occasions, which he supposed might include the funeral of famous, or at least wealthy, sons and daughters of the city.

"And maybe the city's First of July parades?" he said. "Possibly even with you behind the wheel again."

She laughed and brushed the notion aside with one hand. "Never! Never! I cringe to think . . ."

Her attention had been drawn to the few people still working their careful way down the slope. "I imagine your friend would be pleased with all this if he'd known — a large picnic in his honour. My goodness!"

Neighbours and friends, he explained. As well as some merchants from town, and those few city hall officials who still admired the efforts Martin had made in Ottawa on the district's behalf. He did not say that he wondered how many of these people had bothered visiting Martin here while he was alive.

She drifted off in the direction of Martin's house, maybe to see if there was anything she could do to help, or possibly just to be where so many of the women were chatting cheerfully as they continued to set food out on the tables.

Like four little birds on a wire, the young daughters of Ellen and Matt Foreman sat patiently in a row along a thick arbutus trunk that had chosen not to grow upright but to keep its head down and grow horizontally, a metre or so above the ground. Three of the girls swung their feet back and forth, humming some sort of tune, though the one nearest to Arvo scowled and hunched over her folded arms — disgusted, impatient, wondering why she was here.

He had no time to wonder such a thing for himself. Cynthia was suddenly beside him again, a hand on his arm. "She's changed her mind, hasn't she?" She must have been watching, and couldn't stand not knowing what had been said between him and Myrtle Birdsong. "It just took her a little time to get used to it. Did she say she wanted *you* as well?"

For a moment he wasn't sure he'd heard correctly.

Cynthia studied his face, maybe to make sure he wasn't keeping something from her. Then she smiled. "When you drive it down to the city this time, I'll follow to drive you home. You won't want Bert to do it. Lucy might decide she needs another shopping spree and then you'd be at her mercy."

"Instead of being at *your* mercy, you mean?"

"Something like that."

"Do you have any more plans I don't know about?"

"Well. You already know about getting my drive-in theatre up and running again. You think it's a nutty idea, I know, but I still may be asking you for all the help you're willing to give, to keep me from making a total fool of myself. Whenever you're not hiding in your workshop fixing up wrecks. Now watch out, here comes Martin's boy. Probably wants to talk business. I'm out of here! I can't trust myself not to tell him what I think. I remember all too well what sort of boy he was in the classroom. Poor Martin!"

Despite his opinion of this man — and now that he'd resurfaced it was possible to remember the boy he had been, before turning his back on his father — it was only right that he at least *offer* the son a chance to scatter Martin's ashes in his stead. The women had told him this was to be done before they ate. A few people would make brief speeches from the deck, then Ed would start up his outboard motor and take Arvo and the cylinder of ashes out onto the bay. This was something a son might want to be seen doing by those who knew how little he'd done for his father while the man was alive.

But Andrew Glass closed his eyes to the offer, and shook his head. "Uh-uh! No thanks. Just tell me how long this business will take and I'll get out of your way till you're done."

"You don't want to be part of this?"

Arvo could imagine taking hold of this man by the front of his shirt and pulling him up close for a talking-to. "Your father left you his place even though you stayed clear of him for years. You don't think you owe him something?"

Martin's son shrugged. "He wrote me long ago to say the place would be mine. Signed, sealed, and delivered. Guilt, I suppose. Since he knew I wouldn't want to live here I assume he meant I could do whatever I want with it."

"And these fellows with you — this means you've decided what you'll do?"

Martin's son looked at Arvo as he might at any proven fool. "I had the plans drawn up three years ago. As soon as all the paperwork's done we'll start."

"Renovating," Arvo guessed.

"You aren't listening. This old shack will be gone. We've plans for a beach hotel along the base of the cliff." He indicated the cliff that rose behind Martin's house in case Arvo might never have noticed the high wall of weeds and wild shrubbery. "A spa. A pool. A dining room. And — up top in that hayfield, a row of cabins for people who like things rustic. Of course we'll have to convince the government to improve that poor excuse for a road. Tourists want better than that."

Arvo knew there'd be no point in protesting. District officials must have given this man the go-ahead without consulting the community. A meeting would have to be called, a group response determined. Jenny Banks might remember some of her father's speeches.

Earl Boyd had a way of talking to most people as though they were idiots and would probably jump at the chance to take on both the local and provincial governments.

Of course no one in Portuguese Creek had ever succeeded in stopping decisions made elsewhere. Even Martin, though he'd persuaded a majority of local constituents to vote for him, had never managed to persuade anyone else of anything, even after he'd entered the House of Commons. The new park in town may have been his only accomplishment, though even that had been lobbied for by his predecessor.

But you had to try. As Martin himself had said, "You have to try if you want the right to complain after you've been ignored."

"You can tell anyone that owns property along that road they'll soon be rich," said Andrew Glass, his face almost friendly now. "Selling their land to businesses who'll put up shops and entertainment for the tourists."

"That so?" Arvo said. "I know someone who owns a good chunk of land both sides of that road — has her own ideas what to do with it. I wouldn't recommend picking a fight with her."

"She'll change," said Martin's son, turning away from Arvo in order to get on with his important business. "You watch."

Arvo's stomach felt a little queasy. There was no question Martin would have despised this man's plan if he were here. But he wasn't here. He must have known what his son was capable of, yet had done the fatherly thing anyway. He must have known how the community would feel about it, but apparently even an alienated son was more important to a father than his friends. Guilt, probably, as Andrew had suggested.

Could the hotel plans be stopped, and all the touristy stuff that would follow? If the son had official permission to do what he was already doing, this wasn't likely. Of course he may have been bluffing — counting on permission he hadn't yet attained. In any case they could put up a fight, so he wouldn't think he was getting his way without opposition.

Down amongst the driftwood Martin's son was now in a fairly intense conversation with his associates. Maybe they were arguing about whether to leave the place to Martin's friends for today and come back tomorrow. One of them had put on a jacket, or maybe had not removed it earlier. This one seemed a little familiar, even from behind, maybe from the animated gestures.

Of course it was Reynard the realtor. If he wasn't already in charge of selling off any excess land and arranging financing for the hotel, he was probably doing everything he could think of to make sure that he would be soon. He had probably attached himself and his son's Lexus to the tail end of the parade down from the highway.

But there wasn't the opportunity to brood about this now. Myrtle Birdsong was again at his side. "I heard someone saying you'll be scattering the ashes soon."

"I will."

"Well, we can speak again afterwards, perhaps. Or, if not, I'll see you, I imagine, when you are down to return the hearse." She smiled, and stood up on her toes to kiss him beside his ear.

"There'll be a good deal of paperwork to do. Lawyers and what-not."

He knew he would never get to know this woman any better than he did already — a polite but affectionate stranger. Though he promised to return the hearse, he would leave it to her to decide whether she wanted his help with the complicated business of following a paper trail of licenses and documents until it was possible to be certain that no one else alive could claim the hearse. She would have to approach a lawyer who could arrange for ownership to be registered in her name. He may not owe her any obligation to help through this process, but he owed some obligation, he thought, to the hearse — to make sure, if only from this distance, that its future was secure.

There was just one additional thing he wanted settled but this was not the time to bring it up. He could live for a good long while, or he could drop the next time a truck backfired. Eventually he would like to have it written down somewhere that whatever happened between now and then she would arrange for Ben Robinson to drive up here and haul his coffin to the bone-yard in her old man's fancy hearse. After a lifetime of fixing up old wrecks so others could get a few more miles out of them, he would like his final ride to be in something he'd worked on himself. Besides — if he had to go out, he hoped to go out in style.

Of course there would be no question of returning the hearse to the mountain woman now. Her logger sons were better off with the Fargo flatbed, and she would just have to live without her separate sleeping quarters. The realtor, too, would have to accept the fact that his temptations had not won him the eye-catching vehicle he'd planned to park in front of the houses he'd contracted to sell. And now that Martin had been returned to Portuguese Creek and was about to be given a proper send-off, he could no longer lay any claim to the hearse himself — except, perhaps, for another few days while he got it in shape for its journey south.

Cynthia came out onto Martin's deck again to lean over the railing and hammer a wooden spoon against a cooking pot. "Nobody gets any of this food till we've said goodbye to Martin. Where's Arvo?" Arvo raised an arm. "Mario's waiting, down at his boat," she said, and banged the pot a few more times. "But first — *Quiet, please!* — first, there's folks up here who want to say a few words — at least we hope they're few. Then, once they've had their say, and Leena has sung 'Abide with Me,' we'll all head down to the water's edge to watch Arvo set our Martin loose on the sea."

Once the afternoon had faded eventually to dusk and dusk had faded to dark, many of the partiers began to pack up and leave, as Myrtle Birdsong had already done, while those who remained, unwilling to give up on a good time, moved into Martin's house or found a seat on Martin's deck. Fortunately the electrical company hadn't yet been told of Martin's death so it was possible to turn on all the lights and even to play soft music on the CD player. All that remained of the food was brought out from the fridge and the ice chests and set on the kitchen table, the bottles lined up along the counter, for anyone who believed they'd digested their dinner and wouldn't say No to another.

There was no police raid, though one policeman paid a quiet visit some time after 3 a.m. to offer a friendly warning about driving-while-under-the-influence. Those finally trudging up the hill to their cars exchanged last-minute praise for the Martin Glass they were leaving behind in all but memory. Those who stayed with Arvo and Cynthia and the Foremans to tidy up congratulated themselves for having — as Martin himself liked to say whenever someone had been properly celebrated — "done the poor bugger proud."

By the time Arvo and Cynthia were ready to leave, the sun had risen well above the mountain peaks across the Strait and was pouring down morning heat. If any damage had been done to Martin's house it would not be anything serious. No guest had experienced anything worse than a little sand in the eyes, except for the sprained ankle suffered by Billy-boy Harrison, who'd insisted on walking the two-by-six railing around Martin's deck but had stubbed his toe on a protruding nail and jumped feet-first to the ground.

Once Cynthia joined Arvo in the Cathedral hearse for the ride home, she agreed that they had honoured Martin well. "But we don't need to think that this has been any kind of *end*. We've got to rest up for all that still lies ahead."

ABOUT THE AUTHOR

JACK HODGINS grew up in the Comox Valley on Vancouver Island, and taught high school in Nanaimo before moving to teach in the Department of Writing at the University of Victoria. His numerous publications include *Spit Delaney's Island*, *The Resurrection of Joseph Bourne*, *Broken Ground*, and *The Master of Happy Endings*. He has taught writing workshops in Spain, Australia, and Germany, as well as in several provinces in Canada. His work has won many awards, including the Governor General's Award, the Ethel Wilson Prize, the Canada-Australia Prize, and the Victoria City Butler Prize. He has been awarded three honorary degrees, and in 2010 was inducted into the Order of Canada. He and his wife Dianne live in Victoria.

MARQUIS

Québec, Canada

RECYCLED
Paper made from
recycled material
FSC® C103567

Printed on Enviro 100% post-consumer EcoLogo certified paper,
processed chlorine free and manufactured using biogas energy.

100%   PERMANENT